*Katherine's Kingdom:
To Love in Peace*

Book One of the Adven Trilogy

Kathleen Bird

For Miss Noreen,
Kathleen Bird
Philippians 3:14

PublishAmerica
Baltimore

© 2011 by Kathleen Bird.
All rights reserved. No part of this book may be reproduced, stored in a retrieval system or transmitted in any form or by any means without the prior written permission of the publishers, except by a reviewer who may quote brief passages in a review to be printed in a newspaper, magazine or journal.

First printing

Scriptures taken from the Holy Bible,
   New International Version®, NIV®.
Copyright © 1973, 1978, 1984 by Biblica, Inc.™
Used by permission of Zondervan.
All rights reserved worldwide.
www.zondervan.com

All characters in this book are fictitious, and any resemblance to real persons, living or dead, is coincidental.

PublishAmerica has allowed this work to remain exactly as the author intended, verbatim, without editorial input.

Hardcover 978-1-4560-6843-1
Softcover 978-1-4560-6844-8
PUBLISHED BY PUBLISHAMERICA, LLLP
www.publishamerica.com
Baltimore

Printed in the United States of America

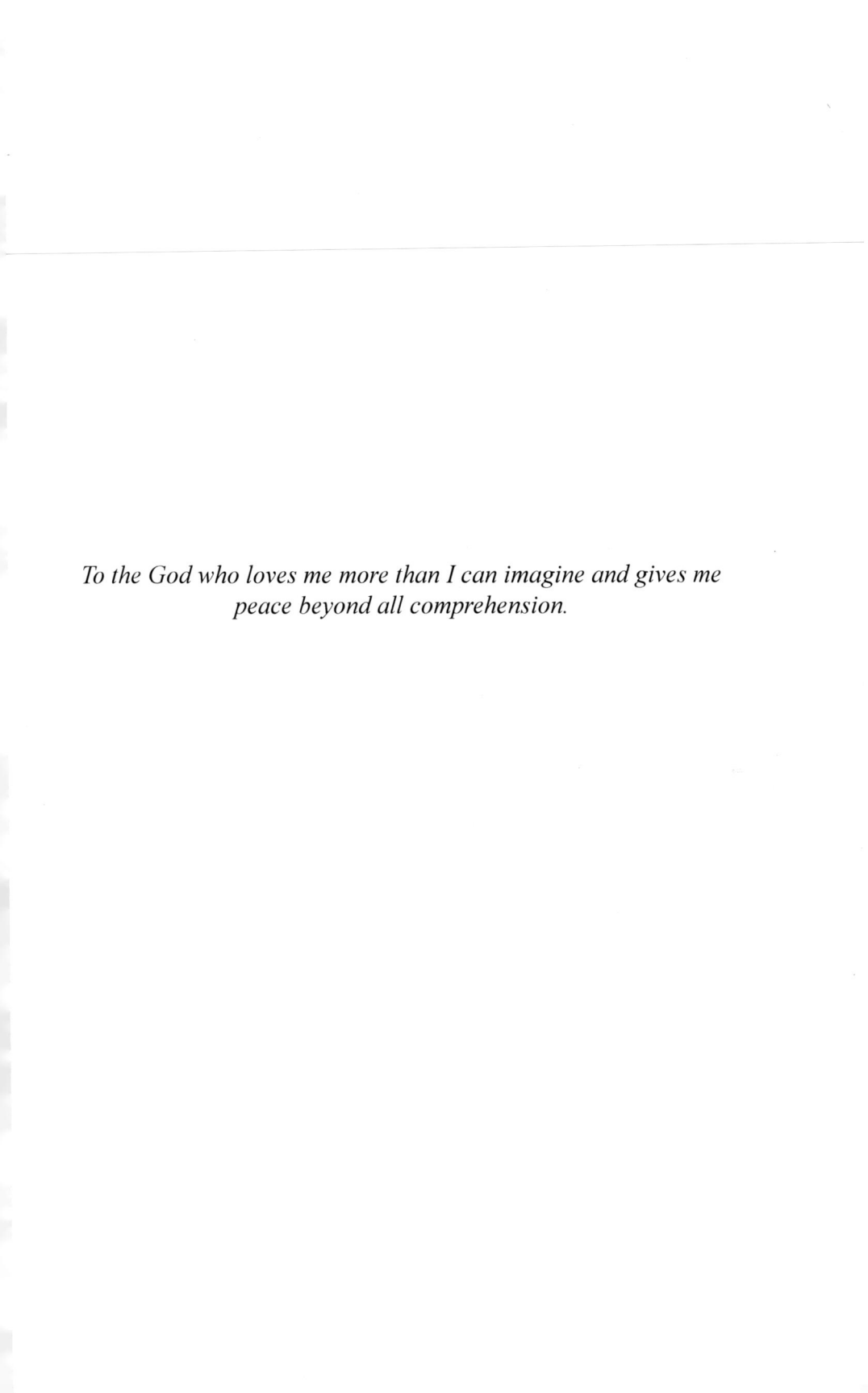

To the God who loves me more than I can imagine and gives me peace beyond all comprehension.

"Place me like a seal over your heart, like a seal on your arm; for love is as strong as death, its jealousy unyielding as the grave. It burns like blazing fire, like a mighty flame."
Song of Solomon 8:6

Acknowledgements:

Thank you to my parents and my sister, who have supported me in everything I've done every step of the way.

Thank you to the many leaders throughout my life who told me I could do it: Mrs. Slater, Mrs. Bunjer, Mary Campbell, Pastor Heath, Professor Brubaker, Pastor Gary and Debbie Fowler.

Thank you to my friends, my biggest fans: Ashley Williams and Sarah Shank.

Thank you to the rest of my family, for all of their encouragement and support.

Thank you to the many people whose smiles make me want to keep writing and whose names are too numerous for me to list.

But, most importantly, thank you to the God with whom all things are possible.

Chapter One

"Your Majesty, there is a message for you."

The princess leapt to her feet. "Is it from my father?"

"No, it is from your sister in Suffrom."

"Bring in the messenger, Eli."

The messenger stepped into the princess's lavish chambers. All the articles of furniture were made of the finest wood in the kingdom. The cloth was sewn by only the best seamstresses. The portrait of the now deceased Queen hung on the wall above the bed.

The princess herself stood next to the bed. She was dressed in a long dress of chiffon, to keep her cool in the summer temperatures. It was a beautiful blue and brought out her fiery eyes. Her blond hair hung down her back in a braid.

"Speak your message, good knight."

"To Katherine, princess of the great kingdom of Adven. From your sister, Queen Ralyn of Suffrom.

My dear sister, all is well in Suffrom. My husband, the king, rules his subjects with justice and mercy. He is much like our father. The peasants work long and will have a good crop when harvest comes in the fall. I have sent Olvin, our finest knight, with a message of joy. I am to have a child! It will come later on in the fall. The doctor has had to tell King Evan a thousand times to let me be. If he had his way I would never leave my chambers. He sends his greetings as well. How is Adven? Is Father well? Evan is worried that you shall become an old maid because I am three years your junior and with child. Calm his fears and mine by sending us news of a wedding. I love you and pray for you and Father every day. May God keep you."

Katherine sank onto her bed. "Little Ralyn? A mother?"

Olvin nodded. "She is quite excited, Your Majesty. She has put all of the castle in an uproar with preparations. She sent me to you at once."

"Thank you, Olvin. Is she correct in saying all in Suffrom is well?"

"Yes, although I can see that not all is well here by the way your face fell when you heard my message was not from your father."

"You must be tired. I shall have a meal and a bed prepared for you. Eli!"

Eli stepped in. "I will have it done as you say, my princess."

Olvin looked at Katherine once before following Eli out the door. Eli closed it and led Olvin through the halls of the castle. There were tapestries on each side and doors that led into other parts of the castle. Every now and then a young servant would run out of one door and into another. Olvin observed that everything was done quickly and quietly. There was no laughter in this castle. He had no chance to stop and talk to anyone because they hurried by him. Olvin turned to Eli.

"Why is everyone in such a hurry?"

Eli sighed. "They think that if they hurry and work hard they will have no time to think of their King, far away in battle, and the princess who waits for a message that never comes. But mostly if they work they will have no time to feel the fear that creeps through the palace walls."

"Is it that bad?"

"I fear it is."

"If King Evan knew he would…"

"I think that is why the princess has told no one. She does not want to worry King Evan and, more importantly, Queen Ralyn. Did you not just say that she is quite excited about her child?"

Olvin nodded in silent frustration.

"Katherine would never forgive herself if she took her sister's husband away just before her child is born."

KATHERINE'S KINGDOM: TO LOVE IN PEACE

Olvin nodded again.

Katherine sat on the chair beside her bed. Ralyn? A mother? It excited her as well as troubled her. She had been considering asking King Evan for more help in the war her father was fighting. She couldn't even think about it now. It would break Ralyn's heart to watch her husband go off to war just before their child was born.

She looked up at the portrait of her mother. "You would know what to do, Mother. I miss you so."

Katherine looked much like her mother. They had the same eyes and hair, but her temperament was nothing like her. She had the fiery spirit of her father and the same skill with the sword. Her sister, Ralyn, possessed the same attitude as her mother, but looked like her father. Her brown eyes and long brown hair looked so much like him that if she had been a boy they could have passed for twins. Aside from this, Ralyn was the image of her mother.

The fiery spirit in Katherine stirred. She stood to her feet and walked to one of the side walls. She pushed a little and a secret door opened. It revealed a room lit by torches along the wall. It was a circular room with a raised seat all along the side. It had no back but was cushioned with pillows. It mattered little to Katherine because its purpose was not sitting but praying.

It was a prayer room. Katherine had it built so that she might pray to the God her mother had helped her discover. He was different from every other god the people of the kingdom served. He was bigger than all of them and yet took time to listen to each of His people. Katherine had led her sister to Him and that was why she was so glad Ralyn married Evan. The kingdom of Suffrom knew God and served Him faithfully. Adven still served the little gods they had served all their lives.

She knelt before her little pew and began to pray. "God, you know how I feel. I cannot ask Evan for help, not now. I am so worried about Father. He does not know you and if he were to die…" Her prayer dissolved into tears.

She didn't know how long she sat there weeping. When she raised her head from the seat, she felt comforted. She also knew exactly what to do.

"Eli!"

Katherine stepped back into her room, closing the door behind her. Eli came rushing into the room.

"Yes, Your Majesty?"

"Have the stable boy ready my horse and have food enough for a month prepared. I am going out to find my father."

"No, Your Majesty! You cannot. Who would run the kingdom while you are gone?"

"I don't run it now. The Regents do. They don't need me here. I must find my father."

"Can you not think about this for a few days? What would I do if you did not return? Who would be heir to the throne?"

"Eli, I have prayed about this already. I feel that I must go, so go I will."

"Does your god send you out to your death?"

"No. He sends me out to find my father."

"I cannot allow this."

"You have no choice in the matter. I am the princess and you are my servant. I have decided."

"Then let me find a companion for you. A strong knight who will protect you from harm."

"I can wield a sword as well as any knight."

"But, my princess…"

The door flung open. A young boy rushed in. Forgetting his manners, he cried out, "A messenger! From the King!"

Katherine rushed past the boy and out the door. She fairly flew down the stairs and into the courtyard. A bedraggled knight stood before them. He was dirty and wet and looked as though he had not slept in many days. He was getting ready to collapse when she caught him.

KATHERINE'S KINGDOM: TO LOVE IN PEACE

"Eli! Get some food and water! Bring them here! Get me a doctor, for I fear he needs one. Good knight, what has happened?"

The knight tried to look at his princess, but could not. He fell back against her. She began to remove his armor, piece by piece, trying to find what ailed him. He was fading fast.

Eli arrived with the food and water. The doctor came behind him. Katherine tried to pour some water into his mouth, but he choked and it ran down his chin. The knight tried to speak.

"Wait, good sir. Rest. Your message can wait."

"It cannot, my Queen."

"You are mistaken, sir. You know not to whom you speak."

"I am sorry that I must die and not be able to explain in depth what has gone on."

"You will live."

"No, my Queen, for Queen you are. Your father lies dead in the field. I myself saw him die. I fled to warn you, for the enemy draws near. Their scouts caught me and I just escaped with my life. I rode three days and nights to reach you, wounded as I was, and now have delivered my message, as much as I can, and may die in peace."

The knight fell back against her and died.

Tears leapt to Katherine's eyes. Father? Dead? It could not be! She remembered him the day he went out for battle almost two years ago. The sky was the most brilliant blue she had ever seen and the grass so green she could hardly imagine there ever being a day such as this one. The knights, with their armor glinting in the sunlight, marched quickly out of the castle gates, eager to do battle. Her father rode before them, his blood red cloak draped over his pure white horse. He had said good-bye to her just before he left, a touching token of his love for her. He left her to rule the kingdom as he would. He told her that when he came back he would expect everything to be in perfect order. Now he would never come back.

The tears fell over onto her cheeks and spilled down her face. She wept not only for her father but for the knight that lay dead at her feet. He had given his life to get the message to her. She felt numb with shock.

"Your Majesty?"

Katherine jerked back to reality. "Yes, Eli?"

"Shall I dispose of the body?"

"Give him the decency of a burial, yes."

He began to walk away.

"Eli?"

"Yes?"

"Send for that horse."

Queen Katherine sat tall in her seat. Her mount was a lovely chestnut brown horse called Genevieve. Draped over the back were her food supplies for a month, along with a blanket. Her cloak and dress were a rich black and fell down to her ankles. Her hair was let loose down her back, the way her father liked best.

Once she set her mind about something there was no turning her back. She would find her father, dead or alive. She would give him the burial he deserved. No one would stop her.

Olvin and Eli pleaded and reasoned with her. "Please, my Queen, do not do this!" Eli begged.

"What am I to tell your sister upon my return?" Olvin asked.

"Tell her all is well in the kingdom of Adven and give her my good wishes on her child."

"But what of you?"

"Tell her nothing."

"But she will surely ask."

Katherine looked at Olvin. He conceded and went to find his own mount.

"Shall I not even find a knight to go with you?" Eli asked again.

"This is my quest and no other's. I will complete it on my own."

With that she turned her horse toward the gate and proceeded out into the countryside.

Chapter Two

For two months she rode through the countryside, avoiding the towns and other people. Her mission was to find her father, not cause a panic. She passed no knights and began to fear she was lost when she heard the clash of battle just over the hillside.

She kicked her horse and sent Genevieve flying down the hill at break-neck speed. As she flew into the heat of the battle, her eyes fell upon the standard of Adven near the center of the valley. Her sword was out in a flash and she began to fight her way towards the flag.

"The Princess! The Princess has come to fight!" The cry rang out through the valley. The knights of Adven were encouraged and began to fight with renewed vigor. Katherine herself felled many of the enemy before they realized whom they fought. At this realization, the enemy scattered leaving only the dead and wounded.

She surveyed the carnage and sent for the doctors before she began to inquire of her own desires. "Has anyone heard of the King?"

The knights shook their heads. One young lad stepped out. "I heard from one of the chieftains that he was slain in battle."

"This I know!" Katherine raged. "Where was this battle?"

The boy shrank back from the Queen's rage and shoved one of his fellows forward. This boy said, "South a piece, Your Majesty."

"Then south is where I shall go."

The knights' faces fell. "Will you not stay to fight with us?" one asked.

"Continue north towards the palace," she said simply and turned south.

Two more solitary days passed. She rode south as fast as she could, looking for any signs of a battle. On the third day she found it. Deep in the woods, the signs of battle were abundant. The dead lay everywhere. It was obvious that the enemy had defeated the knights of Adven. It was a hard loss to them from the looks of it. But no sign of her father.

She had just about given up looking when she found him. A sword had been his demise; she saw. At the sight of him, she wept. His handsome face was pale and his hair matted with blood. That blood red cloak was now dark with its owner's blood. His sword was lying a little ways apart; it must have been knocked from his hand, she thought. The body looked as if it had been trampled over after he died; and it probably had.

The numbness Katherine had felt when she first heard set in again. Until she found the body there was hope that he still lived. Now that hope was gone.

After burying her father, she lay down a little ways away and slept. Her sleep was troubled with dreams of battle and conquest and death and her father and her sister and Adven and Suffrom. A never-ending tumble of pictures and sounds and words:

"Your father is dead."

"I'm having a baby."

"Will you not stay to fight?"

Blood. Blood. A sword. Drawn. Coming at her. The enemy surrounding her. Suffocating.

"You will be conquered!"

Eli! Why is he weeping?

"Katherine is dead!"

No, I am here!

"Her god sent her on a foolish mission!"

No! I chose to come!

The knight.

"You are Queen."

No! I'm not ready! Stop! Why won't the pictures stop! My father's not dead! He can't be dead! NOOOOOO!!!!

She awoke with a start. A sound came from across the clearing. Her hand went to her sword. The rustling sound came closer, closer, closer...

"YAHA!"

"AHHH!!!" Katherine screamed and leapt aboard Genevieve. She drove her out of the forest and into the countryside. Through the dark of night they rode. Just when she felt she had gotten away, she heard the sound of another horseman gaining on her. She tried to pick up speed but Genevieve stumbled and Katherine went flying off her and into the grass.

The horseman approached and she drew her sword.

"Stay! I hold a sword and one should not tempt me to use it!"

The stranger came closer. He spoke. "Who is this who speaks so boldly to the ruler of these parts?"

This angered her. "I am the ruler of these parts! I am Queen Katherine, daughter of Andrew, King of Adven and ruler of the land we now stand on!"

The stranger laughed. "I know not this Andrew nor this Katherine. Perhaps you wish to challenge my claim?"

A glint of steel accompanied his words. It was all the encouragement she needed.

Her sword flashed out, but was stopped by his. "Will you not even allow me to dismount?" A hint of a smile shone through his words.

"Dismount," Katherine replied.

He did so and in one swift movement had tossed her sword across the hill. He laughed.

"You should not let down your guard so easily, *Queen* Katherine."

"Do not mock me!"

"I only give you fair advice."

"I need none of your advice. What do you want of me that you would disgrace me so?"

"Nothing save your name."

"This I have already given."

The stranger walked over and retrieved her sword. He handed it to her. She snatched and sheathed it. He then sat down on the grass and motioned for her to sit down as well. She remained standing.

"Who are you?"

The man smiled. "My name is of no consequence, for I am called many things. The rescuer and the destroyer. The light and the dark. The master and the servant."

Katherine wanted to scream. "I care nothing of what you are called." She again drew her sword and pointed it at his neck. "Only your name."

"My name is King Michael."

He paused as though waiting for her to react to his announcement. He didn't wait long.

"What meaning does that name have that you should look at me so?" Her sword inched nearer.

"I am told it means '*Who is like God?*'"

Her hand wavered. "Are you a believer in the true God?" she asked.

Michael laughed. "Of course I am, for if I were not..." His sword flashed out and he had her pinned to the ground in a moment. "You would already be dead."

He released her and then sheathed his sword. Katherine was upon him in a moment. She threw him to the ground and pointed her sword at his neck. She smiled.

"You should not let your guard down so easily, *King* Michael."

She let him up then sheathed her own sword. They both sat down on the grass, their horses a little ways away drinking from a brook.

Katherine spoke first. "What claim do you have that you are king, Michael?"

"I have no claim except that to my people I am a king. I am king as well as clergy, for my people serve the God that you obviously do, Katherine."

Katherine paused a moment to think about it. Adven was obviously lacking when it came to the spiritual. Perhaps she was still dreaming, and in her dream had entered into another realm, one where this Michael was king.

The thought troubled her. In her sorrow, had she gone mad? What would Eli think?

Michael studied her. She looked like a queen and he had never really ventured out from his own village, his kingdom. Of course, he had never dreamed that a mere girl would come to challenge his claim. He had worked too hard for her to take it away.

But, there was the matter of her faith. She was obviously a believer in God. As easily as he could have killed her, she could have just as easily killed him by now.

Katherine looked at him for a long moment before saying, "How did you come here? *Why* did you come here? How long have you known the one true God? Why have I never heard of you?"

Michael laughed. "I suppose I am a bit of a mystery, aren't I? Well, my story is a long one…"

"I have the time," Katherine said quickly.

He paused. "Well, I came from the kingdom of Suffrom when I was a teenager. My parents had raised me as a believer in God and I decided that God was not for me. Seeing as how everyone in Suffrom believed in God, I ran away. I wanted to be as far away from my old life as possible. So I came here. I, being the naive boy that I was, brought nothing save my horse and was soon starving. The people from one of the villages here saved me and nursed me back to health. I felt awful because I had nothing to give save myself. So I went to work for the leader of the town and soon found that the town had no joy whatsoever. I realized that the only reason I had joy was because of the faith that had driven me away from home. I immediately fell on my face and prayed, asking for forgiveness. God heard my prayer, and I shared it with the leader. He believed and soon the whole town followed. They declared they would no longer be a part of Adven and proclaimed me to be their king, as well as their helper in their new faith."

"How long ago was this?"

"Two years."

The beginning of the war. "How have you remained unscathed by the war?"

Michael shrugged. "God has protected us. What more can I say?"

Katherine thought a moment. "One more question."

"Speak it."

She paused. "Don't think me rude but, aren't you a little young to be a king?"

The sound of Michael's laugh rang through the forest. "I was thinking the same of you!"

Katherine frowned. "I am twenty-one!"

"As am I. I suppose we are young to rule anything aren't we?" He laughed heartily.

"I do not appreciate being laughed at!" Katherine cried.

A noise stopped them both. It sounded like a rustling in the trees.

Michael put his hand on Katherine's shoulder. "Stay here. I will see who it is."

Katherine shrugged his hand off. "I can take care of myself."

With that, she walked quickly towards the forest, with Michael right behind her.

"Who's there?" she called into the night.

Her response was the glint of a sword being drawn.

"Run!" she shoved Michael and raced to her horse. He followed and leapt atop his own mount. They turned them away from the forest and galloped across the plain. The other horseman was right on their heels.

Then the worst happened. Genevieve stumbled. She fell. Katherine urged her to stand again, but the horse was too tired. Michael turned to her.

"Go!" she yelled as she slipped off her horse. Michael hesitated.

"Go," she whispered again as she drew her sword.

Michael looked to see the other horseman gaining on them.

"Your people need you to teach them about the true God," she urged.

"I will come back with help," he replied and sped off into the night.

She turned to face her adversary. He came riding at her with sword drawn. Katherine rose up off the ground to meet him. His sword was crashing down upon her head before she could get fully to her feet. Only her raised sword stopped the assault. He rode past her and returned to try again. She was tired and unprepared to face such an enemy. She fell to the ground seconds before the sword breezed past her. She remained on the ground, her mind fuzzy. The only thing that seemed real was that she was very much alone in a dark forest.

"Help me, God," she whispered as everything faded away.

Chapter Three

When Katherine came back to consciousness, she found herself bound hand and foot in what seemed to be a tent. Her sword had been taken away from her and was nowhere to be found. She sat up to see her surroundings better.

She was indeed in a tent. It was dark and had nothing in it save the blanket she had just been lying on. At one end of the tent was an opening.

A way to escape? Katherine scooted herself along the ground until she could see out the opening.

What she saw was a typical war camp. There were tents for the knights scattered about, and one big tent which must be for their war leader or king. The fire in the middle of it all burned brightly and crackled with intensity. There were several men gathered around it, eating it looked like. A big pot sat by the side of the fire, obviously their supper. The men stood around it, scooping whatever it was into their clay bowls. The men looked thin and tired, but more importantly they were not knights of Adven.

Katherine looked around for their war standard or some other sort of clan marking. Strangely there were none. Not a symbol, flag, or any other mark of family. Also there were no women. That could be easily explained away because it was obviously a war camp, but there should be one or two to cook and clean for the knights.

And there was no way to escape. She could never get past all those men by the fire or any other knight that might be hiding out in his tent.

She sat back and sighed. The ropes chafed her wrists and ankles and she was ferociously hungry. What would these men do with her? She was clearly their only prisoner. What had they done with her horse? Did Michael get away? Were they searching for him right now?

She shook her head. Why was she worrying about Michael? She had more important things to worry about, like escaping.

Just then, a man came out of the big tent. He wore golden armor and a large sword at his side. He was obviously their leader, whoever they were. He scanned the camp until he spotted her.

Katherine scooted back into the tent, struggling to get free. The ropes were tied tight with thick knots; there was no way she could get them loose.

The chief entered the tent and glared at her. She glared back.

"What are you doing here?" he said in the general tongue of Adven.

"Your men captured me."

"Why did you threaten them?"

Katherine's anger boiled over. "I never threatened your men or any of your people! They captured me for no reason!"

He studied her for a moment. Then it seemed like something clicked in his mind. "Where do you come from?"

"Adven."

"Who is your father?"

"My father is dead."

He leaned closer to her. "I don't care. What was his name?"

She closed her mouth and refused to say anything more.

He fumed for a minute and then left without saying another word.

Alone once more, Katherine had a few minutes to think. What did she know? She knew there were a group of unmarked knights just across the southern border of Adven. The chief thought she was hiding something, and there was no way to escape.

She sighed. What could she do? She was their prisoner and there was no way she could get out on her own. Also there was no one to help her.

Michael! The thought leapt into her head before she could stop it. He saw her capture; perhaps he could get word to Eli, or the knights out in the countryside. Maybe his own people would be willing to help her.

What was she thinking? He had probably run off into the forest and forgotten all about her. If she was getting out of here, she would be the one who would have to do it. With God's help, it was possible.

Michael fell onto his bed and sighed. What was he supposed to do? The people were out tending to the crops and he was all alone in the village. This was no time to be sitting on his bed moping. Katherine needed his help! But he had no idea where she was or who the man was who had attacked them.

He stopped for a moment. When had he started calling Katherine by her first name?

Michael shook his head. Again, this was no time for that. He had to figure out a way to help Katherine.

He looked around his house. It was one room, with a fire pit, bed, table and chairs. His sword sat in the corner across from him.

In one stride, he was across the room and his sword was in his hand. "I will find you, Queen Katherine. I will save you!"

He threw open the door and marched into the sunlight.

Michael's horse galloped over the hills searching for Katherine's trail. Whoever captured her was careless. He had left tracks all over the place.

He followed the tracks until he reached a camp. Knights were wandering around the fire and getting ready for supper. The sun was going down and they apparently wanted to eat before dark. Several knights were cooking the food while others put more wood into the fire. Others were cleaning the weapons and feeding the horses.

KATHERINE'S KINGDOM: TO LOVE IN PEACE

Michael crouched outside the camp, hidden in some bushes. He watched all the goings on very carefully. But he saw no sign of Katherine. He saw a rather large tent on one side; that must be where the chief must be. On the other side of the camp was a smaller tent. No one was going in or out of that one.

That must be where Katherine is! They must be holding her as some sort of prisoner! The thought that they were holding her somewhere was enough to make Michael willing to take any risks.

But he had to be patient. "God, please help me. I've got to find her before she gets hurt. Keep her safe until I do."

He drew his sword and crept toward the camp.

Katherine slowly worked to loosen the ropes around her wrists. After she did that she could untie the ropes around her feet.

Suddenly the sound of panicking men and horses filled the tent. She looked out the opening and saw knights running and grabbing their swords and jumping onto horses. An attack perhaps?

"I have come to rescue a friend of mine. I believe you have her."

"Michael!" The ropes slipped free and she hurriedly untied the knots around her ankles. She ran out the opening into the evening sunlight.

Michael stood in the middle of the camp with his sword at the chief's throat. He looked quite majestic as she ran towards him.

"Katherine!" He looked at her with an expression of relief on his face.

But the moment was over too soon. The chief and the knights took advantage of Michael's distraction and began their attack.

Michael swung around and took out several of the knights behind him before turning to face the chief.

"Michael, no!" Katherine grabbed a sword from the nearest knight and headed into the fray.

They fought back to back for several minutes before Katherine insisted, "Michael, we can't fight them all. We must escape while we can!"

"You're right. My horse is behind your tent. When I say 'now' run for it."

"Alright!"

They fought a few more seconds before, "Now!"

They took off for Michael's horse. Brushing past knights and horses, they forced their way out of the fight. When they reached the horse, Michael leapt aboard it and reached down for Katherine's hand. She hesitated.

"Katherine! We've got to go now!"

She glanced back and saw knights with swords drawn coming their way. That was all it took. She reached for Michael's hand and he pulled her up.

"Go!" Katherine yelled and the horse galloped away.

The knights followed for a few minutes before turning back to get reinforcements. They shook their fists and vowed to find them, at least that is what Katherine supposed they were saying. Their tongue was unknown to her.

She held onto Michael's waist as he rode recklessly across the countryside. She had thrown aside the sword she had grabbed, and now devoted her entire attention to staying on the horse. While she thought herself a very fine horsewoman, Michael's eagerness to get away caused his skill to suffer. It was all Katherine could do to hold on.

Suddenly the sound of approaching knights was upon them. Michael paused to look back but Katherine shoved his head back around.

"Keep riding! We cannot outfight them! We must outride them!"

Seeing the sense in her words, Michael urged his steed onward. Katherine listened to the sounds behind them, praying that the knights would tire of the chase and go home. Michael's horse was becoming uneasy because of all the noise and he reared up, almost throwing Katherine and Michael both. The enemy took advantage of the clear shot and an archer let fly an arrow.

"Ah…"

Katherine's gasp startled Michael and he turned to see her falling off his horse.

"Katherine!"

He reached back and pulled her up. She moaned as he readjusted her.

"An arrow struck me. Michael," her eyes looked up at him. "I believe it's fatal."

"No. I'll take you to my people and with God's help they will heal you."

He searched for a glimmer of hope in her eyes but they had gone dark.

Ignoring the obvious truth he slapped his horse and galloped off. The knights were in strong pursuit for awhile but soon turned to go back to their camp. Michael continued his ruthless pace until he reached his home. The women of the village came out to greet him, but seeing Katherine slumped over the rump of the horse, they raced back to their homes to get herbs and medicines.

Michael gently removed Katherine from the horse and carried her to his house. He laid her on the bed and waited for the women to arrive. When they did they shooed him outside and there he sat.

"Dear God, let her live. Please don't let her die!" His prayer turned into silent weeping.

Chapter Four

Eli stood looking out the window. Perhaps she would come home today. She had been gone for over two months now. Would she ever return? *Some people go mad in their grief, perhaps Katherine is one of them.* He shook his head. It could not be so. Katherine was of a sound mind, she would never do that to him.

He looked out the window once more before leaving. He was headed to the temple to offer up more sacrifices for her safe return. But in his heart, Eli knew that the gods he prayed to would never hear him.

Michael paced outside his door. Why was it taking so long? How could it take this long to tell if a woman would live or die?

He forced himself to sit. *They will tell me soon. I must be patient.*

The door opened. The chief nurse came out. He stood. She made a slight bow before beginning.

"The wound is very serious."

"Will she live?"

"We have dressed it as best we can, we must trust God now. He can heal her. I know that he can."

Michael bowed his head. "I know this as well, but do you think she will live? Will God answer our prayers?"

KATHERINE'S KINGDOM: TO LOVE IN PEACE

The woman touched his head lightly, and he looked up at her. She smiled. "The lady will live. I believe that God has great plans for her."

Michael opened his mouth to thank her but she stopped him and said, "And for you as well."

As she turned to reenter the sick room, he sat down on the ground to think.

Indeed Katherine's health was restored and she was moved to the house of the old woman, the chief nurse. Never had the woman had such an avid helper. Katherine was eager to do all the household chores. When the woman questioned her, she merely said that she didn't do much housework at home and wanted to help. The woman sensed there was more, but didn't press her.

Katherine blossomed in the little village as the months went on and the people there grew to love and respect her. But they were not the only ones...

"Katherine?"

She looked up from the clothes she was washing in a large bucket outside her temporary home.

"Michael. What brings you by today?"

Michael smiled. Katherine became healthier everyday and had traded her black mourning clothes for a simple cotton dress. But secretly, every time he looked at her he saw the queen she truly was.

"I wanted to speak with you. Could we sit down?"

"Of course."

They walked over to a fallen tree trunk and sat on it. Katherine looked at Michael and waited for him to begin.

"Well, I...um..." he began clumsily.

"Just say it."

"I wanted to know why you stayed for so long. Isn't there a war on in your kingdom?"

She looked at the ground before answering. "I'm happy here."

"But don't you have a responsibility to your people?"

"I suppose they think I'm dead already."

"People who love you will never forget you or take you for dead. Don't you have any family?"

Her thoughts went to her sister, Ralyn and her baby on the way. Also King Evan and Eli. Eli! He must be worried sick about her!

"Yes," she said. "But they can find someone else. I don't want to go back. I want to stay here." She looked at Michael. "With you."

Michael coughed. "I…um…I…" He sighed. "Katherine, I would love for you to stay here with me and my people forever, but we both know that you must go home. God has placed you right where he wants you, and that is in Adven. Please, don't do something we'd both regret. Go home, Katherine."

With that he stood up, ignored her protests and left. Only when he was out of sight did he allow the tears to fall down his cheeks.

Eli gently pushed open Katherine's door. It was somewhat dusty, but it looked just the same as the day she left. Her mother's picture hung on the wall as though it was looking after things in her absence. Her clothes were lying on the bed, thrown hastily by their mistress. All things reminded Eli of Katherine and his heart ached at the thought that she had been gone five months now. Ralyn's child would be born in a few months, and the war continued to rage on. What Adven needed was its queen, but its queen had seemingly disappeared.

He ran his hand along the wall feeling the wood and praying as best he could. He had no time to offer sacrifices today; perhaps the gods would listen to his prayers instead. The priests said the gods must be offered sacrifices in order for prayers to be heard but maybe this once…

Abruptly, his hand felt nothing but air. A small gap in the wall became apparent. Eli was startled, but curious. A secret passage perhaps? What did the princess need with a hidden door? He shoved a little and the door opened enough for him to step into the room hidden behind the wall.

He took in the torches and the long bench with cushions. *What is this?* Eli thought. It was then that he noticed something shining on one of the cushions. He walked over and picked it up.

KATHERINE'S KINGDOM: TO LOVE IN PEACE

He instantly recognized Ralyn's careful stitching. On the deep purple fabric the silver thread stood out. Inscribed on the pillow was the following:

I hereby proclaim,
To all who may find this room,
That I have found the One True God.
He has saved me from eternal death
And I am forever grateful.
May you, whoever you are,
Find him in this place.
~ Katherine, Princess of Adven

Eli stared at the pillow. He knew that Katherine had discovered a new God, but he never knew about this room, or about the fact that Ralyn knew about Him. What was she thinking? How could she abandon all of Adven's traditions for a God she knew nothing about?

Then a thought occurred to him. He could test this new God. If he prayed for Katherine's safe return as quickly as possible, and it was answered, he would know that this God was real.

Eli gently knelt on the floor next to the bench.

"Oh great God, may you hear my prayers and answer them! May you, by your great power, bring Queen Katherine home to me and let her lead all of Adven to peace."

Unsure of what to do next, he stood up and quickly walked out of the room. As he closed the secret door, he offered one last plea, "Please?"

Katherine sulked around the house for the next several days. She was angry at Michael and she was angry at God. Why would he offer her peace and happiness and then steal it away? How could Michael try and force her to leave?

"I thought he loved me!" she yelled to no one in particular.

"He does."

Startled, she turned around to see the old woman standing in the doorway.

"Maria! I didn't know you were there."

"Obviously."

Katherine went back to sweeping the small kitchen, but Maria wasn't done with her yet.

"Katherine, Michael only wants the best for you."

"How did you...?"

"I know many things. But the most important thing right now is what you know."

"What does that mean?"

Maria came closer and stopped Katherine's frantic sweeping. "It means that you must know in your heart that Michael loves you and that God loves you."

"I do."

"Do you?"

The simple question was enough to bring tears to her eyes. Katherine tried to stop the tide, but it was impossible. "I have to do the right thing don't I?"

Maria nodded.

"Even if it means I have to give up something?"

Maria nodded again. "You have to go where God tells you, Katherine. You must go home."

Katherine opened her mouth to say something, but then closed it. She sighed before quietly walking out the door.

Maria went and sat down in her chair and began to pray.

"God, help her to follow you. She wants to but she needs help with her unbelief."

Katherine walked stiffly across the village on her way to Michael's house. She didn't want to leave but she knew that she must. Adven needed her.

Michael was sitting on his bed deep in thought. He had denied food for three days, ever since he had spoken to Katherine. He had tried to help hadn't he? He tried to do the right thing, right? Why should he have to give up his love for her in the first place?

And so he had spent the last three days fasting and seeking God. He knew he should speak to her again, but he was distraught. He loved her. Why should he have to give her up?

A knock on the door surprised him. It was probably Maria telling him to eat. He started to tell her to leave when he heard his name.

"Michael? Are you in there?"

"Katherine?"

"Yes. I'd like to speak to you."

He opened the door and stepped out. "Yes?"

"I'm ready."

For a moment Michael was confused. "For what?"

"To go home."

His heart soared and he pulled her close to give her a hug. They stayed that way for a minute before he said, "I'll come with you."

Katherine pulled away. "What?"

"I could never be happy without you so I'll go with you."

She stood stunned so Michael continued. "Katherine, will you marry me?"

Her tears of joy and another hug were his answer.

Chapter Five

The wedding was a grand affair. Gold and purple flowers were hung from the trees and long vines were draped across the openings. Michael appointed one of the older men to do the ceremony since he himself could not. He wore his best clothes and a fine purple cloak with a gold chain. His sword was fastened at his waist, ready for battle. But Katherine herself was the most beautiful bride. Her dress was a shimmering white and it was so long that it dragged on the ground. To solve this two little village girls were appointed to carry her train. Her blond hair was let down so that it would flow almost to the ground and there were more gold and purple flowers braided into it. She also wore a purple cloak with a gold chain that fastened around her neck, just above the neckline of her dress.

The lovers exchanged their vows and then a great feast was held with music and dancing. People sang praises to God and thanked him for his kindness to give them such a just king and a loving queen. A crown was placed on Katherine's head and she was declared queen to rule beside Michael. The new husband and wife ate and danced together and had a thoroughly wonderful time. As everyone was going home, Maria approached them with a gift.

She bowed low before them to give them honor before she presented it.

"My king, I have nothing to offer you but my service. I hope that that is enough."

Michael smiled. "You owe me nothing, Maria."

She nodded. "But, I do have a gift for my queen." She extended the package toward Katherine.

"Thank you, Maria," Katherine said before opening it.

Inside the package was a lovely sword obviously made of the finest metal. On the hilt was carved flowers of all kinds. But it was the sword itself that interested Katherine.

"What do these words mean?"

Maria smiled. "They are words of a very wise king. He was very much like yourself."

"I am not a King."

"Not here." The unspoken meaning left a sense of sadness in the air.

Michael broke it by saying, "What does it say?"

Katherine turned the sword so that she might read it and read aloud.

Place me as a seal over your heart,
Like a seal on your arm;
For love is as strong as death,
Its jealousy unyielding as the grave.
It burns like blazing fire,
Like a mighty flame.

The words wrapped around the sword like a vine. They were etched into the metal itself, and they shone like polished gold. All in all a curious gift.

"What do the words mean, Maria?" Katherine asked again.

She said nothing.

"Maria?" Michael prodded gently.

"They mean two things. On the surface they speak to the love of a husband and wife. For you, it means you must remain faithful to one another. Keep your love afresh and renew it each day. Your love must be so strong it conquers death."

"And the second meaning?" Katherine inquired.

"It speaks of the love of God for his people. His love is a fierce and jealous love, but far stronger than any kind of love we might have for each other. His love burns in you like a fire and spills over into your actions. If you continue to follow him always he will continue to bless you." Maria bowed. "May this sword take care of you in the battle that you must now undertake, My Queen. Let it never leave your side and you will have great success, but do not forget the lesson I have taught you. God bless, Queen Katherine."

With that Maria left the two lovers standing in awe and what had just conspired. Michael looked at Katherine, and she at him. Neither said a word. All was still for several moments before she spoke.

"We must leave at once."

Michael took Katherine's hand. "I am eager to leave as well, but we must have time to ready enough supplies for the journey. I promise we will leave in the morning."

Katherine looked at the sword. She studied the words a little longer before sheathing it and tying the belt around her waist. "I am ready now. Let us leave in one hour."

She walked away to begin the preparations. Michael watched her and smiled.

"What kind of woman have I married?" He shook his head. "A foolish but wise one." And he followed after her.

The horses were readied for the long journey and loaded down with enough food to feed an army. Michael and Katherine had thought they would be going alone, but several of the young men insisted on joining them.

"How could we call ourselves your servants if we left our King and Queen to return home without an escort? We are at your service." With that, the young man bowed low to the ground and the rest of the men with him.

Michael stepped down from his horse and took the man's hands in his own. "Rise up, no one is worthy of such devotion save God himself. But, if you are in earnest you are welcome. Do not think you are required to give me service of any sort."

The men rose up off the ground with smiles on their faces. "We only hope to accompany you to keep you safe. Queen Katherine must be brought home to her own people safe and sound."

Katherine smiled down at them. "I can wield a sword as well as any man. Do not think that I am in need of your protection."

"As you wish, my queen."

Michael held up his hands for quiet as the laughter spread through the ranks. With a nod from Katherine, Michael smiled and said, "All who are willing to come are welcome indeed. But we are ready to leave now."

"As are we!" the men cried as they tried to contain their brilliant smiles.

Michael looked helplessly at Katherine as she too tried to keep from smiling. With a defeated gesture, he mounted his horse and off the whole party went.

The group moved slowly, for while Katherine had resigned herself to return home she was in no rush. The young king and queen allowed the group to move at a leisurely pace, rest often, and eat much. Two weeks after they left, they came to a familiar grouping of trees. Katherine became sullen and would speak to no one. Michael tried to convince her to talk to him but she wouldn't. Often she went off by herself to pray she said. Unfortunately, she came back more angry than before. No one could understand why she was acting so strangely. The men tried to comfort her; they played songs and games by the fire every night. Nothing would console her. She remained morose and distant.

Michael was becoming desperate, he begged her to confide in him; but she refused. He urged her to tell the men to hurry on so they might be away from whatever it was that troubled her. She responded by ordering them to stop. So for two more weeks they stayed by this certain grove of trees and impatiently waited. Michael stopped asking Katherine what bothered her and spent his nights with his men. After a fortnight had passed, he spoke to Adam, the young man who led the men following the king.

"What am I to do with her, Adam? I've tried everything, and I don't know what else to do."

"She still refuses to speak of what's troubling her?"

"Yes!" Michael stood to his feet and paced around the fire. "I have begged, pleaded, and I am simply worn out with worry over her." He sat down. "Why won't she speak to me?"

Adam leaned over his friend and replied, "Why don't you try to speak to yourself?"

"What are you talking about?" Michael stared at him as if he had gone crazy.

"Think to yourself as to a reason Katherine would be so upset by this place. Do you know the reason without asking her?"

Michael thought hard. Then he sighed, "Adam, the only thing that happened in this place is Katherine's kidnapping and our first encounter. She is no longer in danger from the kidnappers, and I would think that our meeting place would bring about happy memories. Why does it fill her with distress?"

Adam sighed as well. "I do not know, my King, but at least you have a starting place to work from now."

Katherine tossed and turned in her bed. Michael lay sleeping soundly beside her, oblivious to her misery. The nightmares filled her head with words and pictures.

"Your father is dead."

"Katherine is dead!"

"Her god sent her on a foolish mission!"

"You are Queen."

The words flowed together in a confusing tangle.

"Where do you come from?"

"Adven."

"Who is your father?"

"My father is dead."

"An arrow struck me, Michael."

"People who love you will never forget you or take you for dead."

"I thought he loved me!"

"They are words of a very wise king. He was very much like yourself."

"I am not a King."

Images of her father,…bleeding, dying,…Michael, what is wrong? The image of her father was replaced with the image of her husband.

No! Michael, don't die! I need you! I love you!

GOD, WHERE ARE YOU?!

Snap!

She awoke in her bed with Michael still sleeping beside her. The men outside were snoring and all was peaceful.

The prayer at the end of her dream echoed through her mind.

"God, where are you?" The tears flowed down her cheeks and soaked her pillow.

Michael stirred and rolled over. He lazily opened his eyes, yet seeing his wife crying sat up wide awake.

"What's wrong? Katherine, are you hurt?"

She wiped her face and shook her head. "It's nothing, Michael, go back to sleep."

He watched her as she rolled over and tried to go back to sleep.

"Sleep well, my love." Michael kissed her and lay back down.

Katherine muffled her sobs in her pillow.

Chapter Six

The next day Katherine went out into the forest once again. She was searching, always searching. She couldn't find it and it troubled her. She sat on the ground sobbing pitifully until it grew dark. Why had she forgotten so quickly?

Michael thought and thought and thought. He could think of nothing other than what he had told Adam. Why did this place trouble Katherine so? Why couldn't he figure out what was worrying her?

As he stormed out of his tent in time for supper, he noticed Katherine wasn't back yet. He slumped down beside Adam who was eating and laughing heartily.

"How can you laugh at a time like this?"

Adam turned to him. "A time like what?"

"This!" Michael angrily replied.

"You still cannot figure out what is wrong with her?"

In answer, Michael stood up and stormed back into his tent. After a few minutes, Adam followed him.

"You must not be so worried over her. She will tell you when she is ready."

Michael sprawled on his bed and looked at Adam. "I have to worry. She's my wife and the queen of my people, and her people as well! How can I pretend nothing is wrong and go on with life?"

Adam sat on the bed beside him. "I am not saying that. I am merely suggesting that you wait patiently for Katherine to tell you whatever it is that's bothering her. She will tell you. It just may take some time."

"We don't have time! Winter will be here in a few months and we must reach Katherine's people before then. She is being ridiculous."

"No wonder you cannot understand her problem!"

Michael looked at him, his eyes were trying to form a question.

Adam sighed. "What I mean is simply this: you cannot understand her problem until you understand her. Has she been mentioning anything that might suggest she is angry at someone or something? Or has she been acting lonely or homesick? Besides her forest visits is there anything else that would suggest the cause behind her moodiness?"

"No, except…" Michael trailed off remembering how Katherine had awaked as though from a horrible nightmare last night. "I think she might have had a nightmare last night."

"What about?"

"I don't know."

"Do you have any idea at all?"

"I don't know, Adam."

"What about…"

"I said I don't know!"

Michael's violent outburst startled himself, as well as Adam. He groaned and sat up. "I'm sorry, Adam. It's not your fault. I'm just so worried about her."

"My King, please wait and ask her yourself tonight. She will tell you, I am sure of it." Adam stood up and walked to the door of the tent. He turned back to face Michael. "She will tell you. I trust God that she will."

Michael nodded and lay back down on his bed. "I will ask her when she returns. I will know then. She will tell me."

Sleep overtook him and he drifted into a dream.

Katherine stood to her feet, ready to give up the search for the night and go home. Maybe she was being foolish. They should go on. Eli would be waiting for her. She should forget her past and move on.

It was at that point in her musings that she realized it was very dark and she was very far from the camp. The wind blew through the trees and made her shiver.

"Where am I?" Katherine said to herself.

The trees all looked eerie and mysterious. The branches seemed to reach for her as she walked past them. The wind moaned as it whistled through the tree limbs. Everything frightened her and she was eager to be home in bed with Michael.

Then suddenly it hit her.

"I'm lost!" she cried out with dismay as she saw that her wonderings had carried her so deep into the trees that she would never find her way out.

"Someone help me! It's me…Katherine! Michael?" her cries trailed off as the tears overtook her. "Please someone help me…"

"Your Highness? It's Adam. You must wake up. Katherine is missing."

Michael groaned and rolled over to face Adam. "What is it now, Adam?"

"Katherine hasn't returned yet. No has seen her since early this morning."

Michael jumped out of the bed and grabbed his sword. "We have to find her. She could be anywhere. Why haven't you left yet?"

Adam put up his hand. "There is more. One of the watchmen saw a large gathering of people to the east. They looked like a very large war camp."

"What is their country of origin? Their standard?"

"There was none to be found."

Michael knew instantly who they were. "It's imperative we find Katherine immediately." He pushed past Adam and mounted his horse outside.

KATHERINE'S KINGDOM: TO LOVE IN PEACE

Adam followed him and mounted his own horse. As he pulled up alongside Michael he asked, "Why?"

"Her kidnappers have returned." Michael said gravely. He swung his horse around and they headed into the forest.

Katherine turned around in circles, not wanting to stray far from her original spot. The trees all looked the same and they haunted her. Images of her father stalked her every move and she wished with all her being that she had not insisted they stop. The nightmare rang through her head, clear as a bell, even though she was not sleeping. How would she ever make it stop?

Exhausted, she slumped to the ground. "Will I never make it home, God?" Her tears began to flow again and she wiped them away. "I don't have time for that! I'm a queen of Adven, and queens don't cry! At least, I don't think they do."

Right then Katherine felt very much like a lost little girl. She wished with all her heart that she could curl up in a little ball in her mother's arms and cry for hours on end. She didn't feel like a queen or a wife or…

"I certainly don't feel like a mother!" Katherine rubbed her stomach, ever so gently. "Michael doesn't even know. What will he say? He'll be happy of course, but he'll smother me." A smile crossed her face. "Ralyn's baby should be due soon. Our children will only be a year apart perhaps." Katherine scrunched up her face and thought hard. "None of it matters if I don't get home."

With that she stood to her feet and began walking in circles again, making as much noise as she could.

Michael's horse shied at the thought of entering the dark forest. Michael coaxed him onward and ordered Adam and his men to follow him. Adam and Michael led the men deeper and deeper into the forest, calling Katherine's name over and over, hoping to hear her voice in response. They searched the trees trying to catch a glimpse of her dark blue dress blowing in the wind or her blond hair capturing the light of the moon. Michael's thoughts whirled with her. Every picture his mind had ever had of her flitted through his thoughts. The men scoured the forest. No corner was left unturned. Michael was close to despair when they heard a wailing over the increasingly loud wind. A woman's shrill wail pierced the night.

"It's her! It's Katherine!" Michael cried out over the wind. "Over to our left! Find her!"

Adam led the men into the howling wind and the now pouring rain. They found Katherine huddled on the ground over a little mound of earth. She was wailing inconsolably. The rain soaked her dress and her hair and still her tears streaked her face.

"Father! Father! How could I have forgotten! How could I ever forget?" Her cries echoed across the forest.

Michael dismounted and ran to his wife. "Katherine! Katherine!"

The wind whipped her hair into her face. The tear streaks stained her cheeks and her blue eyes looked at Michael mournfully. "He's dead, Michael. Father's dead. I never got to say good-bye. He never met my God. Our God, Michael. He never met Him. He died and I never got to tell him I loved him!" She collapsed weeping into his arms.

Michael held her and kissed her wet hair. Her moans subsided eventually. She buried her face deep into his chest and fell asleep. Adam cried out over the wind and rain, "We'd best be getting her back to the camp! Who knows what those other knights are planning."

He helped Michael lift Katherine into the saddle, trying their best to not wake her. She was in a deep sleep and didn't stir, even though they jostled her quite a bit. The wind howled and the rain poured, but Katherine stayed asleep. All the way back to the camp she slept. And as Michael and Adam carried her to her bed, she slept a sleep so soundly nothing would have woken her.

Katherine awoke to the sound of packing. The whole camp had been torn down while she slept and the only thing left was her and Michael's tent. The men stood in groups talking and laughing. The horses stamped their feet impatiently while the men finished their breakfast.

She scanned the crowd looking for Michael. He stood off to one side, watching the work and listening to Adam. He held the reigns of his horse and rubbed her nose with his other hand. His eyes danced from one person to another, observing the work and the interaction between them. Occasionally he would nod in response to Adam.

Then he saw her. His eyes ceased their wandering and watched only her. They reflected his joy at the sight of her and his concern for her wellbeing. Adam noticed that his King was no longer listening to him and stopped talking. Gently he took Michael's horse from him and led her off to the other horses. Michael barely noticed, but began to walk towards his wife, his Queen.

Katherine shifted her feet nervously. How could she explain? She hadn't told him about her father, about the reason she was out here in the first place. She hadn't spoken to him about the reason she was reluctant to head home. Why should he even trust her? She shook her head. He was her husband, the love of her life. Of course he would understand. He understood her didn't he?

"Katherine, you're up. Did you rest well?"

She nodded.

Michael hugged her. He didn't say anything more; but then again, he didn't need to. He knew she didn't need comfort, she didn't need a lecture, she needed his love.

Katherine let herself fall completely into his embrace, soaking in his love. The time would come, she promised herself. She would tell him, but for now she would stay here, wrapped in her husband's embrace.

The group moved off, hurrying its pace to make up for lost time. Michael and Katherine led, laughing and talking like nothing was wrong; but Michael knew. He knew something was wrong, the way she had been acting wasn't her. Although she had returned to her normal self this morning, he knew that something had happened last night. He would have to ask her about it, and it would have to be soon. He glanced quickly behind him, but the strangers were no where in sight.

The men set up a temporary camp for the night and cooked a hurried supper. Katherine sat off to one side, eating quietly and thinking to herself.

I must tell him soon. He must know, about Father and the baby.

Her thoughts were interrupted by Adam. "My Queen, are you well today?"

"Yes, thank you, Adam."

He sat down beside her. "The King was worried about you yesterday. Where did you wander off to?"

Katherine stared at the ground.

"Your Highness?"

Not a word.

"Katherine?"

She looked up and their eyes met. "Katherine, whatever is wrong can be mended. Give it to God and confess it to Michael. 'Cast all your cares on me,' says our God."

Katherine nodded and stood up. "Thank you, Adam. I will talk to Michael now."

As she walked quickly away, Adam smiled. "God, what do you see in this girl who is trying so hard to be woman?"

Michael stood on the other side of the camp watching and observing. When he saw Katherine rise up and come towards him, he turned and walked a distance away so they could speak privately. She came up and touched his shoulder.

"Michael?"

He turned and looked her in the eyes. "Katherine."

"Michael, I suppose you wonder what happened yesterday."

"The thought did cross my mind."

"I wanted to tell you why I was in the woods all those months ago. My Father had gone off to war two years ago. I waited anxiously for a letter from him, but it never came. Finally, I heard that he had died. In my grief, I tore out on my horse to find him, to prove it wasn't true." She moved closer to him and looked straight into his eyes; the tears spilled onto her cheeks. "It was awful…" The tears overtook her and she collapsed.

Michael pulled her close and for the second time that day just held her.

That night Michael slept fitfully. He knew that his wife was sleeping better than he for the first time in months. Time moved slowly toward daybreak, and still he hadn't slept at all.

As soon as it was light enough, the group moved on. They moved quickly, yet with caution, aware they may be followed. Scouts patrolled the road before and behind. They gave no sign of intruders. Michael watched Katherine. She looked much better than two days ago, and gave no sign of her former trauma. Still, he watched her and she watched him. There was something else, he was sure of it.

"Michael? Is something troubling you?"

He shook his head and smiled at Katherine. "No. Just eager to get you home."

"Home. I think I'm finally ready to go home."

She got a faraway look in her eyes and then smiled a silly smile at him. Perhaps that was all it was. She was homesick, was that what he felt? Michael shrugged off the feeling. Katherine was homesick, that was all.

Chapter Seven

They covered a lot of ground in the next two weeks, and the time passed quickly. It was a time full of joy and laughter, but underneath simmered worry. Autumn was well on its way, and winter was fast approaching. Michael urged them onward, while Katherine hung back in the shadows. Outwardly, she insisted she longed to go home, but everyone knew that she would not begrudge them any time. She spent a lot of time talking to all of the knights, everyone became her friend. The men enjoyed the familiarity, but Adam saw it as avoiding Michael. Perhaps there was still more that Queen Katherine was not telling?

"Your Majesty?"

She jumped up from the place she had been sitting. The tree stump was that of an ancient oak, chopped down not long ago. "You startled me, Adam!"

"My apologies."

He sat down on the stump. Katherine looked around for any other surprises. The sun shone brightly down on the autumn colors. The grass was dry, but the trees were alive with color. Red, purple, and brown leaves tumbled onto the path in front of them. The wind blew gently, brushing stray hairs from her face. She pulled her braid to be sure the wind had not loosened it. Adam sat solemnly on the stump, watching her every movement. The wind rustled through his brown hair and his bright green clothes.

"Did you come to ask me something?"

"No. Did you have something you wanted to tell me?"

She shook her head and continued studying her braid. The gold in her hair contrasted sharply with the dullness of her surroundings. Adam smiled. It seemed she always made her surroundings duller than she herself was.

Just as he was about to say something else an arrow whizzed through the air and struck one of the trees behind them. Adam grabbed Katherine's arm and dragged her away as more arrows flew at them.

"Michael! Michael!"

Michael came flying out of the tent at Adam's call. When he saw Adam dragging Katherine along behind him, he rushed to his wife's side. "Katherine! Are you alright?"

"I'm fine," she said, shaking loose from Adam's grip. "But, the knights we saw. They are…"

"Right here," came the voice of the chief as he stepped from behind Michael's tent.

Michael drew his sword to protect his family and his people, but the chief stepped forward with his own sword drawn. "I wouldn't do that. You are surrounded." As he spoke the knights with no standard stepped out of the shadows. They immediately disarmed the knights trying to protect their King and Queen and rounded them up. They stood with their hands bound behind their backs in the center of the camp. King Michael and Queen Katherine stood beside the chief with their own hands bound and their weapons taken, including Katherine's marvelous sword. Adam was set apart, as a sort of hostage. He was guarded by two guards twice his size.

"It is so nice to meet you again, milady." The chief walked around his prize and examined them as if they were horses. He was still wearing the golden armor, creating as much of a contrast with their surroundings as Katherine's hair. "And you sir, caused quite a stir in my camp when last we met. Isn't it nice that I am able to repay you in kind?" He laughed at his own joke. Michael shook his head.

"Do you disagree?" The chief edged his sword closer to Michael's throat.

"Don't hurt him!" Katherine's frantic cry amused the kidnapper.

"Do you think I'd hurt him so soon in the game?" He laughed his derisive laugh again. "Besides, what is he to you?"

Michael took a step closer to Katherine. "She is my wife."

"In that case…" The chief hit Michael in the stomach with the end of a stick he'd been toying with. The King crumpled to the ground. Katherine knelt beside him and put her cheek against his, since her hands were tied. Adam growled a warning to his guards to be wary.

"How sweet! The little wife taking care of her husband," he mocked.

"What do you want?" Katherine asked.

The chief paused his mockery for a moment to consider her. "I know who you are. You are little Andrew's daughter!"

"You knew my father?" The wonder in her voice was beyond comprehension.

"I was his servant. He treated me like one too. I told him one day I would be a great king and he would be my servant. Your father disliked me and threw me out. Now I have come back to prove him wrong. Too bad he had to *die* and ruin my fun. Oh well." At this point, he ran his finger along Katherine's chin. "I'll still have his daughter for a servant."

"I would never serve you!"

The chief slapped her hard across the face. Confusion reigned for a moment as Michael stood and tried to attack the chief, sword or no sword. The guards rescued their chief and gave Michael a black eye for his trouble. Katherine scolded Michael with her eyes.

"See how pointless it is to resist? We outnumber you ten to one."

Katherine was still upset. "You'll need every one of those men to defeat my knights."

He laughed. "*Your* knights, is it now? Are you so calloused to your father that you take his throne so readily?"

"I loved my father!"

"Loved, you say?"

KATHERINE'S KINGDOM: TO LOVE IN PEACE

Katherine was silent.

"See?" he laughed. "I was right. You love his throne more than you loved him."

"That's not true!" She wrestled with the ropes around her hands, but they were far too tight for her to get free.

"You are nothing more than a little girl doing a man's job!"

Defeated, Katherine slumped down and pressed her eyes shut to keep back the tears. The guards yanked her and Michael to their feet; and the company and the captives moved out.

Late that night, when the moon was hidden from sight and they were deep into the woods, the chief called for a halt. The captives fell asleep where they sat and the knights soon followed. Only Katherine and Michael dared to stay up and talk.

"Don't listen to him." Michael tried to see Katherine's face in the dark, but couldn't.

"I didn't want to, but he's right. I don't even know what I thought, trying to be Queen of Adven. I'm not even a good wife to you, Michael!"

"Of course you are!" He drew closer to her, still searching for her face in the dark.

"No I'm not!" Muffled sobs were heard.

"Katherine, do you remember what Maria told us before we left?"

She thought hard, then whispered, "No."

"Place me as a seal over your heart, like a seal on your arm; for love is as strong as death. I've set you as a seal on *my* heart, Katherine. I would love you if you were the worst wife or the worst queen. *My* love for you will go beyond the grave, should we not make it out of this place." His face found hers in the dark and they kissed. For a moment they stayed, wrapped in each others' love and loyalty, then Michael pulled back. "I know that you loved your father the same way, no matter what anyone else says."

"Perhaps you're right. I just don't know what to think anymore."

He felt the conversation ending, but there was still so much to say.

Katherine awoke to someone pulling on her arm. "Michael?"

The face leaning into hers and grabbing her arm was not that of her husband. The rough knight dragged her to her feet by the elbow. Her foot kicked Michael as she struggled to stand. He was awake in an instant.

"Where are you taking her?"

The knight did not respond. Katherine struggled to come fully awake. The pain in her arm helped immensely.

"What's going on?" The knight dragged her further away, regardless of the fact she was still not awake. Her dress caught in the leaves and loose branches along the ground. Her wrists hurt her because of the ropes, and her head was quite foggy. Rough hands grasped her elbow and pulled her through the brush. The sun was not up high enough to provide much light, so they fumbled through the dark. Her blond hair fell in her eyes in loose strands from her braid, and she felt like falling on her face.

When they reached their destination, the knight flung her to the ground. Katherine got to her feet with a great effort.

"Sleep well, my slave?"

The chief grinned wickedly at her. Katherine glared back.

"I thought I was your servant."

"I decided 'slave' was more appropriate. A servant might be set free." He shoved his finger in her face. "A slave is mine forever."

She was bustled out of the tent before she could say a word. The silent knight dragged her back to Michael and dropped her, as if she were a sack of garbage. Michael scooted close to her and tried to brush the dirt from her hands and face.

"What happened?"

Katherine shook her head. "I don't know. I suppose he just wanted to remind himself that he really captured me… and remind me that I'm in his control."

He sat back and thought a minute. "Perhaps he's trying to break you. You're more useful to him if you've given up."

She laid her head against Michael's chest. "He won't succeed. I won't break, unless he takes you away from me." Katherine turned and looked into his eyes a moment. "Nothing will break me as long as I'm with you."

At that moment, Adam and several others of their number were dragged from sleep and tied to the horses of the other knights. They let it happen without a fight, for Adam had advised it would only cause more trouble and waste their strength. Another knight came and grabbed Michael by the arm, who surprisingly gave no argument. The same silent knight from before came and grabbed Katherine.

A little fear pierced her heart as she watched Michael be led away. "Where are you taking him?" She started to follow him, but the silent knight pulled her back. "Let me go! Michael!"

His solemn face turned and met her frantic gaze. "For love is as strong as death," he whispered. Then the other knight roughly turned him around and tied him to the last horse in the party, the one piled high with luggage.

Katherine followed her captor to the front most horse, that of the false king and kidnapper. Her rope was tied to his bridle; and she was left to her own devises. The hustle and bustle was carrying on all around her. She watched as Michael's people were tied to horses, mostly one at a time. Perhaps it was their way of ensuring there was no easy escape. Adam was farther back in the line, somewhere in the middle, and Michael was at the very end. Just then, a most unpleasant person came up beside her.

"Well, my slave, what do you think of my army?"

The men were more numerous than she could ever imagine. Had there been this many last night? She shrugged.

"These are the men who will overrun your father's palace, *your* palace. At least, it was yours, before I captured you. Now you and all of Adven are forfeit to me!" He smiled at the wonder of it all. "And to prove how great I am, I will ride with you tied to my saddle at the front of the procession. Perhaps there will be no fight when they see I've got their precious queen." He mounted his horse, and kicked Katherine to be sure she was paying attention. "I never realized the true genius of this plan. My slave, I do hope you're used to walking; we've a long way to go."

With that, he flicked the reins and the whole troop proceeded forward. The false king picked up the pace, while Katherine ran along the side of his horse.

The sun beat down on the dusty trail. There was no breeze to speak of and the air was stifling hot. Katherine took long deep breaths to keep from passing out. Her ragged sleeves were covered with her perspiration, as she wiped her face again. The hem of her dress was in tatters and her shoes were falling apart. Blond hair fell in and around her eyes, releasing tears from their aggravated state of indecision. Trees leaned out threatening branches across her path; and more than once, she stumbled and fell.

It was the same as it had been for a week. Day after day, she was up before sunrise and dragged to the chief's tent. After he ridiculed her, she was tied to his horse and forced to run along the side of the road to keep up with his life threatening pace. The men behind her were forced to do the same. The days where they had sat around the fire, laughing and singing, seemed ages ago, but it had only been a week. Everyday Katherine struggled to pray for wisdom, and a chance to escape. The chief looked down at her from his high perch.

"Still denying that I've won?"

Katherine said nothing.

"There's no use hoping for escape. Winter will come and go before you are set free."

A brightly colored leaf fell in her path, as if to punctuate his words. Fall was fading quickly before her very eyes.

"I do not intend to attack before winter. You see, if, for some reason, I didn't win right away winter is not my choice season to fight a war. It's not my brother's choice time either. He's the leader of the tribe that you've been fighting with for the past two years."

Katherine froze. Fear and panic seeped into her every being. Then anger, boiling hot, rolled over into her mouth and before she knew it she was shouting at the top of her lungs. "It's your fault my father is dead! If he had never fought this war, he'd still be alive!" She whirled around, causing the horse to falter in its step.

"I wouldn't do that if I were you." The voice came from behind her. A face, that of the formerly silent knight, peered around into hers. He flashed his sword in her face and then shoved her roughly to the ground.

"Don't damage my slave!" whined the chief. He tugged on the rope attached to Katherine and used it to pull her up like a fish on a line. She was so mad she couldn't speak. The light had not only reflected off the bright metal of the sword; it had reflected off the words, "It burns like blazing fire, like a mighty flame."

Alone with her thoughts, separated from her friends and her husband, Katherine fumed. She tried to calm herself, to concentrate on something, anything else, but that evil man was responsible for her father's death! It was his fault! And he had the gall to give her sword to one of his ruffians.

Michael was hidden away from her view, the same as every other night for the past week. Her heart ached to see him. Why did she not tell him everything right from the start? Her pain was almost physical, it hurt so badly. The sick feeling in her stomach was no help either.

She prayed earnestly as she clutched her tumbling stomach. Nausea was attempting to overcome her, but she would not give in. Love welled up in her heart for Michael, Adam, Ralyn, and Eli. And as the nausea subsided, love sprouted for this new little one inside her. She only hoped his mother would be a queen, not a slave, when the time came for him to enter the world.

"I suppose I don't even know it is a boy," she murmured, but she was interrupted by a youth of about sixteen years bringing her food.

He cautiously set the plate in front of her and then sat down. Katherine refused to eat while he sat there. The staring contest continued for a long while, before the boy stood and leaned close whispering, "I am a friend. Please eat."

She looked at him suspiciously. He nodded eagerly. "I was enlisted by my father, not by my choice. He bargained with the chief, who promised my father much land if I would fight. I tried to tell my father it was wrong, but he would not listen. 'Adven was not meant to be ruled by fools,' he said." He paused. "I'm sure he wouldn't have said that if he'd met you, milady."

Katherine sized the boy up. He was tall, skinny, and very pale. The only color in him at all was his red hair, the color of fire, which stuck in every direction from lack of care. While he spoke, his hands were never still. They played with the stones on the ground, the leather on his boots, and the hilt on his sword. It was the sword that made her nervous. Unarmed, she stood no chance against this boy, feeble though he was.

" I didn't want to fight this silly war. I liked your father. I thought he was a great king. Please," he struggled to find more words. "Please believe me. I just want to help you." He looked at his hands and forced them to be still.

"What is your name?"

"Edwin."

"Edwin, I must ask you to do something for me."

His voice reflected his excitement. "Anything, Your Majesty."

"Hit me."

His face fell. "What?"

"It won't do to have someone suspect you're helping me. Act like you're upset because I didn't eat. Hit me! Yell at me! Do whatever you want, but make a scene!"

Edwin stared at her. His face looked like she had asked him to cut off his right hand. In another moment he drew back his hand and slapped her cheek hard. Her head snapped to the right, and she almost toppled over. He was yelling in some other strange language and gesturing wildly. Several men turned to see the abuse and snickered. Katherine held in her tears of pain as Edwin returned to his seat. His hands did not return to their former activity. They were too busy shaking.

Chapter Eight

Another day passed. Katherine trudged along beside the chief. He talked on and on about himself and his plan to conquer Adven. It was enough to give her a headache. When they finally stopped for the night, she collapsed and fell instantly asleep. Her next conscious thought was that of someone shaking her awake.

"Queen Katherine. Your Majesty. Please wake up! Please!"

She tried to concentrate on the speaker, but her eyes blurred from exhaustion. It was Edwin, looking nervously about and shaking her frantically. His eyes darted from side to side like a caged animal. His voice raised in pitch when he spoke again.

"Please, we must go now! I overheard the chief speaking to his second in command. He is angry that you won't succumb to his power. They plan to kill your husband!"

"Michael!"

She tried to calm the panic swelling up in her, threatening to engulf her. "We can't be hasty. What about the plan? Did they say when?"

Edwin continued to shake and looked at the ground. Katherine threw herself at him, grabbing the front of his cloak with her bound hands. "Tell me what they said!" she shouted.

Her shouting woke up the men sleeping around the fire. They ran to Edwin's aid, pulling her off of him and dragging Edwin away. He shoved off their hands and shouted in the strange language. Then he shouted at the men holding Katherine as she struggled on the ground. They instantly let go.

With strength she didn't know he had, Edwin grabbed her and pulled her off the ground. He shouted in her face, his tone sounding angry but his words giving instruction.

"I think they were waiting to give you one more chance. Be ready to go at anytime, I'll warn the others. They're keeping your husband in isolation, so I won't be able to warn him. Keep safe, I'll keep up the act."

With that he dropped her roughly on the ground and stomped away. Katherine sat staring at him as the men laughed. Just exactly who was this young man she'd befriended?

Another day marched slowly by. Katherine's feet ached and she shivered from the slight chill in the breeze. Leaves cluttered the path and the sky hinted at rain. Her day was made worse by the fact that she didn't know what would happen to her. Would he really kill Michael? What would happen to her if he did? What would happen to the baby?

The chief glanced down at her. "You aren't walking fast enough!" He tugged at her rope and dragged her forward. The motion made her wrists bleed and she fell to the ground. She couldn't take much more of this. Katherine dusted herself off and trudged onward. The wind played with the leaves on the path making them dance as they reminded her of the oncoming winter.

Night came quickly for all. The moon rose steadily upward as the night grew chill. Katherine felt she had only been lying down for a few moments before someone roughly shook her awake. Her vision was fuzzy as she tried to concentrate. "Michael?"

"No, it's me. Edwin. It's time."

Realization grasped hold of her. She tried to stand, but was too tired. She collapsed back to the ground in defeat. Edwin grabbed her gently by the arm and stood her to her feet. The sword in his hand cut neatly through the rope. He thrust it into her hands. "You might want this."

She gazed down and her eyes filled with tears. The fine script and interwoven designs were those of her own sword. "Thank you, Edwin."

"We must leave soon, Your Majesty."

Cautiously they crept across the camp. The leaves crunched as they walked, and the sound seemed to echo around the emptiness. Edwin touched her shoulder to direct her.

"I will get Adam and the others. Your husband is behind that tent over there." He pointed off to her left. Katherine nodded and moved off in that direction. The darkness of the night surrounded her, making the stars above twinkle like tiny candles. The leaves swirled around her feet, and the branches of nearby trees swept down in front of her path. When she finally reached the place Edwin had indicated, she gasped in horror.

Michael lay on the ground, slumped over as if he was dead. His hands were bound and his wrists were caked with blood. In his beard were remains of dried blood and bits of leaves. His hair was mussed and tangled. His clothes were ragged and torn. Katherine gently set her sword on the ground and knelt beside him. Her hands ran over his face, which was more black and blue than anything else. His eyes were swollen shut, so she softly rubbed them to reawake the muscles. He moaned slightly and tried to sit up.

"Sshh, Michael." He turned his face towards her and struggled to open his eyes. When he did, his eyes filled with tears.

"Katherine…"

"It's okay. I'm here."

He sat up and let out a groan.

Katherine put her finger to his lips. "We're getting out of here. Edwin is getting the others, just follow me."

"Who?"

She grabbed her sword and cut the ropes around his wrist. "Don't worry, he's a friend." Quickly, she pulled him to his feet. They started out across the clearing, with Michael supported on one arm, and her sword in her other. Edwin met them in the middle of the camp, surrounded by Adam and the others. They looked only slightly better than their king, who was struggling to stand next to Katherine.

Edwin grabbed Michael's other arm and helped to support him, while Katherine readjusted her sword hand. She turned to the others and opened her mouth to speak, when suddenly a cry sounded out in the night and the alarm was raised.

"Move!" Katherine cried and dragged Michael forward with Edwin following behind. Adam and the other men trailed behind, struggling to keep up. The whole enemy camp seemed to come alive. The fire was lit to light the way, and the men poured out of their tents. They stormed the woods, with the shouts of their chief in the background.

Suddenly, Katherine stopped running. Edwin fell forward, bringing Michael down with him. "Your Majesty! What are you doing?" Edwin gasped, as he lay panting on the ground.

"Just keep going. I'll stop them." She reached out her hand to help them up.

Adam stepped forward. "You can't do it yourself. I'll stay to help you."

The sounds of the enemy were coming closer, almost upon them. There was no more time to argue. Katherine whirled around, with her dress spinning around as the wind picked up. Her sword was pointed out in front of her as the warriors pressed in before her. Her eyes burned with anger and the sword felt hot in her hand.

Suddenly, like a flash of lightning, fire burned from the sky to the sword in her hand. The light filled the night, almost as if it were day. Men fell before her as though they had been struck down. Katherine was blinded for a moment, but when her sight cleared, the enemy lay on the ground, alive but set back. The sword went slack in her hand as she stared at it.

Edwin was the first to recover. He cried, "We must go!" Adam grabbed Katherine and pulled her along as the party sped off into the night.

Hours later, they were far away from the camp. Everyone collapsed on the ground, thoroughly exhausted. Katherine lay back against a tree trunk. Her eyes fluttered as she tried to concentrate. She focused her attention on the sword in her hand. The words twisting around it, the moonlight glinting off the metal. It mystified her.

Fatigue swept over her. The mystery was too daunting to solve tonight. The men were lying around on the ground, sleeping where they fell. She walked slowly over to Michael, laid her sword on the grass, and went to sleep.

The sun rose later than usual. The wind rustled the leaves that brushed through the sleeping men. Slowly, one by one, they awoke to the sudden realization that they were very lost. For weeks, they'd been wandering, following someone else's roadmap. Now, they knew where they needed to go, but not where they were.

Adam immediately took charge of the situation. "We must gather everyone together. Perhaps someone will have an idea of where we are."

Edwin nodded. "None of us knew where we were going. We were simply following orders. Maybe someone was tracking our location better than I."

Michael sat up. He was the weakest one of all. Being forced to go behind meant he dealt with keeping up the ragged pace and walking in ruts left by the others. The enemy warriors had also been the cruelest to him, and the chief had given specific instructions for torture. The quiet king refused to talk about it, but it was clear he had grown stronger in the last few weeks. His eyes were quick and alert. He stroked his scraggly beard and thought. "Katherine, I don't suppose you know where we are?"

She shook her head. "I wasn't paying enough attention. I'm afraid I've never been very far from the castle in any case."

The group was quiet for a moment. Katherine found it hard to think about their current problem with last night's still unsolved. She ran the scenes through her head over and over, but without luck. The puzzle was too great for her to solve alone.

"Adam. Edwin. Gather the men. I'll speak to them in a moment." Michael's voice was firm and unwavering. The two men quickly left to their tasks. Katherine walked to where her husband was sitting and sat beside him.

"You aren't thinking about our problem, are you?" His voice was kind and concerned. Katherine's heart broke.

"I'd almost forgotten what your voice sounded like." Her speech was inhibited by the tears filling her eyes.

He pulled her closer to him. His hand gently touched her face as he turned it to face him. Katherine leaned her head on his shoulder to avoid looking at him. "I've missed you."

Michael let his hand drop. His eyes looked out across the woods and the trees. They studied the sky and the clouds drifting past. The leaves whistling through the trees danced lightly upon his vision. Short blasts of icy wind hit him, causing him to shiver. When he had sufficiently studied the surroundings, he gently moved Katherine off him.

"You can't stand up!" she protested. Her hand shot out to catch him as he stumbled. "You're still weak."

"No weaker than any other man. We've all been through the same. I must speak to them and find out where they think we are."

"Michael…" Katherine's voice trailed off as she watched him fully stand and take a few steps. His steps weren't sturdy enough to convince her, but she did not object. Slowly, he walked past her and she trailed along behind him. Her stomach felt like it was tied in knots.

The men stood in as close a semicircle as they could, considering they were in the middle of a forest. Michael and Katherine stood in the opening, waiting patiently for quiet. When the noise finally died down, Michael spoke up.

"Men, we are glad to be alive and free today." Cheers erupted. Katherine gestured for quiet. "Many thanks to this young man, Edwin, who has rescued us." Edwin blushed. More cheers. "And to God, for saving us." This time the cheering lasted for a lengthy amount of time before Katherine was able to calm them. "But, winter is fast approaching, and so is the enemy. Even now, they are probably searching for us on their way to the castle. The man in charge has an agenda. He wants to destroy all of us, and especially Queen Katherine." She noted the use of her title. "We must move quickly if we are to save her and all of Adven. However, for the last few weeks we have been wandering aimlessly according to the will of a lunatic." The men began to murmur among themselves. "And now we have lost our way. But, with God's help, I pray we will find our way again." Cheers. "I must ask. Does anyone have any ideas as to the direction we should go?" There was silence. The men looked at each other and the ground and anywhere but Michael. Katherine felt all was lost.

Night fell again. The stars glittered above as it grew chill. The men wrapped themselves in whatever they could find to keep warm. Luckily, no snow fell. Katherine drew close to Michael and whispered in his ear. "Your speech was wonderful."

He sighed and rolled over. "No one knew anything. Now what do we do? Those men are probably on your doorstep by now."

She tried to comfort him. "We'll figure it out. There must be some way."

He turned to face her. "Isn't there anything you remember? Anything that looks slightly familiar?"

Tears filled her eyes. Michael was desperate and frustrated and it was all her fault. "No. I wish I did." She paused. "Please don't be mad at me, Michael."

His eyes softened. "Why would I be mad at you?"

Her stomach rumbled.

"I don't know where we are."

"No more than any of the rest of us."

"But, I should. I'm the queen aren't I?"

He laughed. "And I'm the king."

She frowned in the darkness. She could feel his smile laughing at her. "Of these men, yes. But, I'm supposed to be queen of all of Adven…and…and…" Her anger dissolved into silent tears.

Michael was instantly serious. "Katherine, there's nothing to be upset about. Many nobles have never been beyond the four walls of their castles. It's not your fault we're lost."

She sniffed. "But, it is. If I hadn't been with you, we wouldn't have been kidnapped. Actually, if I hadn't been with you, you wouldn't have been heading for the castle at all. And…"

He stopped her. His finger pressed gently on her lips. She felt his emotions overwhelm him. Her heart beat faster as he spoke. "If you hadn't been with us, I would have never met you. And if I had never met you, I wouldn't have been the luckiest man alive." She opened her mouth to object. "No. Don't say anything else. Just go to sleep. God will work it out for the best."

With that, he lay down and fell asleep. Katherine wrestled with sleep for a bit longer before giving in.

Chapter Nine

The sun broke through the doubts of the night before with its bright sunshine. The little warmth it brought awakened the sleeping knights, along with their king and queen. The brightness brought hope and refreshment to the tired men. As they packed up what little they had, they laughed and talked. The sunshine brought more than the day; it brought the promise of a new start. And so, they started off through the forest, hoping and praying they were going the right direction.

Katherine's feet hurt. The past few weeks of walking had made callous upon callous, but that still did not prepare her for those next few days of constant walking. Her wrists were still healing and her dress was so thin it did no good against the cold. Michael walked beside her, helping her in rough parts. He stood straight and tall, seemingly unaffected by the cold. The men followed behind, with Adam and Edwin in the front, directly behind the king and queen. The sun lacked all hint of sunshine; it was as ice cold as the wind. Still there was no snow. That was the only good news.

"Can we stop for a moment, Michael?"

"We need to keep moving. I want to cover more ground today."

"But…"

All it took was a look from him to silence her argument. But in a moment she had recovered her courage. "I'm tired, Michael. Can't we rest for just a moment?"

"No. We don't have much time before it starts to get too cold to walk. The snow will stop our progress and we won't reach the castle in time."

She had had enough. "It is my choice whether we stop or not. It is my castle we are trying so desperately to reach, and it is my kingdom we are trying so desperately to save. I say we stop."

He turned to face her, frustration evident on his face. "Then let's give up all together because if we stop now there's no point in going on."

"I don't want to stop for the day, just a moment."

"Then you'll want to stop for the rest of the day, then the next day, and the day after, and before you know it, winter will be upon us. All is lost after that."

Katherine stomped her foot. "You're overreacting. None of us have eaten properly for weeks. We're dirty, tired, and thirsty. Just because you can keep walking for days on end does not mean the rest of us can. If you would just…"

"Your Majesties!"

The couple stopped fighting long enough to face Adam.

"It seems we all need a rest. Edwin, find a good spot for us to stop." Edwin bowed shortly and led the men off to a clearing a little ways away.

"We must keep moving, Adam. It's like I said…"

"Enough," Adam said sternly.

The king stopped. Katherine crossed her arms. "If he would just listen…"

"I said enough." She stopped.

"No matter what the situation; it is never appropriate for kings and queens to argue with one another in front of their subjects."

"It's his fault…"

"She contradicted me…"

"Stop!" The talking ceased.

"Now, what is the matter with you two? You've barely spoken. If I didn't know you, I would say you were two complete strangers."

Edwin entered the circle of conversation. "Everyone is settled. Is there anything else I can do?"

Michael's countenance stiffened. "This doesn't concern you."

Katherine snapped back. "Don't talk to him that way!"

"I can talk to him any way I want to."

"He's my friend!"

"I'm your husband!"

"Maybe I wish you weren't!"

"Well, I'm sorry you can't change it!"

"Katherine! Michael!"

The two stopped and looked at Adam.

"You are being ridiculous. Stop this fighting immediately. There are more important matters to worry about. After all, you are the king and queen."

"Well, maybe I don't want to be queen after all!" And with that, Katherine stomped off.

Michael huffed into his beard and marched off in the other direction.

Adam and Edwin stood looking at each other. Several moments passed in silent contemplation. "We ought to go after them."

Edwin sighed. "I suppose. What do you think got into them?"

"I wish I knew, Edwin. I wish I knew."

Katherine laid back and tried to relax. The ground was cold against her back. Tears streamed down her cheeks. Her whole body shook with shivers and sobs. She rolled over onto her stomach and buried her face in the leaves. The dirt was wetted by her tears as they splashed onto the ground.

Crunching leaves coming from behind startled her. She sat up and struggled to draw her sword. Edwin raised his hands in surrender.

"You shouldn't...*sniff*...sneak up behind someone."

He sat on the ground beside her. "I'm sorry if I made the situation worse. That wasn't what I intended."

She sniffed. "It wasn't your fault. Michael wouldn't listen to me."

"That still doesn't give you the right to argue like that in front of the men."

"Well…" she stopped. "You're right."

"And if there's a problem between you and Michael, you need to solve it."

"There's no problem! Who said there was a problem?"

Edwin looked at her with one eyebrow raised. She sighed. "It's not his problem…it's mine."

"You need to solve whatever it is."

She stood up and walked away from him.

"Katherine, Your Majesty."

"Please go away, Edwin."

"But…"

She turned to face him with tears streaming down. "I can't solve it in a moment. Please leave me alone for awhile."

"What do you want, Adam?"

Adam said nothing but continued to stand beside Michael. Michael pounded his fist on the tree. "She wouldn't listen to me! Who gave her the authority to talk to me like that?"

"Her father."

Adam's wisdom was infuriating. "Well, I'm the king."

"Not yet you aren't."

Michael glared. Adam spoke, "When we reach her people, she will be in charge; not you. That's weighing heavily on her. Just give her a chance."

"She's had her chance. She won't trust anyone."

"Now who are we talking about? Katherine or you?"

Michael sat on the ground. The wind whipped his hair around his face and blew leaves into his beard. The scraps he called clothing chilled him to the bone as temperature dropped. He sighed heavily. "I don't know. I don't know her. Maybe I never have."

Quietly, Adam sat down beside him. His face was full of contemplation. After a long while, he spoke. "I think you know her better than she knows herself."

"That can't be true. I spend more time talking to you than I do her!"

"Katherine's hurting. How would you feel if you waited for months and months to hear from a father you adored and who suddenly is gone? What would you do if you were told in the same breath that your father was dead and you were queen? How would you deal with seeing your father lying dead on the battle field?"

"Okay, Adam. I get the point. But, none of that is my fault."

"It's not her fault either, but she thinks it is."

"Is that all it is? She's blaming herself for things out of her control?"

Adam nodded. The wind blew the first hint of frost in their faces. Leaves rustled in the trees and danced along the ground. The more brittle ones broke into minute pieces.

With that, Michael stood to his feet with grim determination on his face.

He marched through the men resting around the fire and past the trees on the outskirts of camp. Adam winked at Edwin as they watched Michael marching along. But, when he reached the edge of camp and saw Katherine sitting on the ground, he stopped and leaned against a tree. The wind was blowing her hair and revealing her tearstained face. The braid had long ago come undone, allowing her blond hair to blow in all directions. Her arms wrapped around her knees and pulled them closer to her body. At her side, the sunlight glinted off her sword.

Michael gathered his strength and marched onward. She barely glanced at him. Mustering what little courage he had, he sat down beside her. Nothing was said. The two simply looked at the trees seeming to grow on the horizon forever.

"None of this is your fault." Michael's voice was very quiet and gently reassuring.

"Yes it is." Her tone wasn't argumentative, simply stating a fact.

"Only if you let it be."

"How is it not my fault?"

"You didn't kill your father."

Silence. A tear slipped down her cheek.

"I mean…you would have stopped him if you could…"

"But, I couldn't. I couldn't stop the war. I couldn't stop him…I couldn't save him…I…I couldn't save him."

"It isn't your job to save people. It's God's."

"I couldn't save you…or Adam…or any of the men…"

He was losing her. Michael reached over and took her hand. "But, you didn't have to."

Katherine looked at him. "What do you mean?"

"Well, your sword. You didn't do that, did you?"

She shook her head and picked up her sword to study it. "No, I remember feeling angry because they were chasing us. And, I picked up my sword, but then there was a flash and someone grabbed me… Then we were running away; and I don't remember any more."

"The point is, *you* didn't save us. God did. He just so happened to use the sword in your hand."

"But…"

He pulled her closer. "No buts. God saved us. It had nothing to do with you."

She flung her arms around him. Her tears dripped onto his hair and his neck. The sobs were muffled in his shoulder. Then suddenly, she stopped.

"Katherine…Katherine…Is everything okay?"

He pulled back to look at her. The tears were still falling down her cheeks and onto her dress, but her face was filled with a look of ecstasy.

"Michael!" She stood up quickly and started to run away. He grabbed her hand.

"Katherine! What are you do…?" He saw what she saw.

In the distance, silhouetted against the sunset with its oranges and yellows and purples and pinks…was the castle. The flag of Adven flew from every tower. Faintly, he could here the neighing of horses and the crying of babies.

Chapter Ten

Katherine's feet were fairly flying. Home was within sight. She could almost feel the baby within her jumping for joy, or maybe that was just her upset stomach. The men were staring at her, but as she raced through the camp Adam and Edwin were motioning for the others to follow. So, they all were running through the forest toward their final destination: the castle. Michael had finally caught up with his wife, and so they both ran side by side.

It had been too long. Katherine's God must not have heard him either. Every day, Eli would sneak into her room and pray behind the secret wall. He stopped offering sacrifices to the other gods because he thought Katherine's God might become jealous. But, nothing he had done seemed to work. The war still dragged on, more knights were returning home to find no end in sight and no leader to finish what had been started, and Katherine was no where to be found. With each new face, he questioned and begged and pleaded and hoped to hear word from her. But, still nothing.

As was his usual habit, he had gone into her room, pleaded with her God, and then walked out on her balcony to look at the road. Every afternoon it was the same. Today would be no different. He would wait a few minutes to watch the coming and going, what little there was, and then return to his usual duties.

Out on the road, he saw some bedraggled peasants running up to the castle. He could hear them laughing and shouting. They were dirty, as though they had been running all night. This late in the day, the gates would certainly be locked. Perhaps he should go down and let them in, just to hear what news they might have.

Eli walked slowly down the hallways. He nodded politely to the women tidying up the rooms and the cooks in the kitchen making dinner. The warriors were repairing some weapons in the courtyard; and the stable boys were taking care of the horses. But, there was quite a commotion at the gate.

"Please, you must let us in!" a man's voice was calling. He sounded exhausted. "My wife…"

"Let me speak to Eli! Let me speak to Eli!" The woman's voice was excited and high pitched. It sounded familiar.

The warrior at the gate was motioning Eli to him. He was clearly unsure what to do.

"Let them in. Perhaps they have some news."

Quickly, the gates were opened and the visitors poured in. They were all men, plus one woman. Clothes were ragged and torn, looks were just as ragged. They were all undernourished and thin. The woman was standing next to what must have been her husband, the leader clearly by the way the others watched. She was talking excitedly and asking for him, Eli.

"How can I help you?"

"Eli!" The woman's blond hair flew around her face as she rushed to hug him. "I've come back. I have so much to tell you. I…" She paused to look at his face. "You don't recognize me?" She shifted the sword at her waist.

Eli thought for a long time before answering. "Who are you?"

Her face fell. "It's me. Katherine?"

"Katherine?" He studied her face. The eyes were the same. The voice. The tousled hair. It really was…

"Katherine!" He threw his arms around her and swung her around. Every gray hair on his head stood up in happiness. "Where have you been? Oh it doesn't matter. You're here!"

Michael stood by Adam and Edwin, quietly watching the scene unfold. When she had satisfied her happiness, Katherine turned back to them.

"Eli, there are a few people you should meet. This is Adam and Edwin, both have been of great help to me these past few months. And this is Michael." She slipped her hand in his. "My husband."

Eli stood in silent shock. "Your husband?"

She nodded. Michael waited before responding. Adam and Edwin simply smiled.

"You went off and got married? I have been waiting for almost seven months for you to return home and *responsibly* lead your people while you ran away and married some vagrant in the forest!"

Adam frowned and prepared to fight. It felt odd for the rest of the men to watch so helplessly, with no weapons, while their king was ridiculed. Edwin fidgeted and glanced at his new found friends. He had just escaped from fighting a war; did he have to start another so soon?

Michael turned his head and put out his hand. His slight movement held back the more fidgety of the men, but they were still anxious to defend their king's honor. He then turned to Katherine. Would she stand and watch this man slander her honor as well?

She sighed. "Eli, I shouldn't have left. I should have stayed to rule the kingdom like you wanted me to. But, I'm here now! I've come back to do what is right. God protected me and…"

"Protected you? Yes, you are alive, but you are dead to me. You know the expectations of a queen. She is to marry someone of high royal blood. That man is to be responsible, honorable, and a good leader. A man wandering through the forest *cannot* have any of those qualities. As for these others…" He waved his hand at the other men. "They can be no better. I am grateful for your life; it would have been too much for Ralyn to lose both father and sister in the same space of time. And yet, she still has lost something…" Quickly he turned and walked off. He didn't say a word or turn back to give other directions, no final good-bye.

Katherine's eyes were full of tears. The man she respected most, other than her father, had just disowned her. What had happened to this place? What had happened to the people she cared most about?

Michael put his arm around her. He felt like he had let her down. "Perhaps we should have waited. This is my fault. I shouldn't…"

"No, I wouldn't want it any other way. You *are* responsible, and honorable, and a good leader. Eli, will learn to trust you; just like I trust you."

They hugged. A cheer rose up from the men. Yes, they had expected a better reception, but they were still here. Safe and finally home.

The door creaked a little, but not a whole lot. Perhaps someone had been in here recently. Her mother's eyes looked down at her, welcoming her home. Katherine knew that she would have been proud of her. She had found her father and given him a formal burial. She had found a man who loved her and would protect her, and Adven, for the rest of her life. She had found a people who loved God just as much as she did, who would help her lead Adven to the new hope found in Him. Lastly, she had found herself. She had discovered who she was and what was important to her. Right now, Eli loving her again was her top priority.

Dust floated in the weak sunlight. The bright spring sunshine she had last seen in this room was long gone. Now winter was quietly sneaking in. That bought her some time before that madman of a chief returned to claim his war.

Katherine sat down on her bed, causing more dust to fly. This place held so many memories. So many happy moments spent with her mother, her father, Ralyn, and Eli. But, there was that last day. The last day she was here. The place now left a bittersweet taste in her mouth. Her father's death had broken a part of her heart; and she wasn't sure she could ever repair it.

Sadness and sorrow overcame her calm mood. Overwhelmed, she collapsed on her childhood bed and sobbed.

Knock. Knock. Knock.
"Come in."

The door opened to a very plain chamber in the castle. The windows were covered so they blocked all sunlight. Various manuscripts and official papers were strewn across the floor and the bed and the night table. Michael tread very carefully across the floor, trying not to step on anything of value. A solemn form was slumped over the table. It was too quiet.

Michael stopped to look back at the young servant boy who had led him to the room. The boy simply motioned him onward. Eli sat up slowly and looked with mournful eyes to see his visitor.

"Get out."

No response.

"What do you want? You've already stolen her away from me. I raised that girl like my own child!"

"Eli, I've brought her back to you, to her home, to the whole kingdom."

"You kept her away. Seven months! The war could have been lost by the time you brought her back."

"But, it wasn't. We have some new information that might be of use to you and the army as well. Won't you give me a chance?"

Eli thought for a long moment and rubbed his long white beard. His eyes searched Michael's looking for a clue or a hint as to his motives. When he found nothing to discourage him, he said, "What is your name?"

"Michael, Prince of Suffrom."

Eli's eye rose. "I know the King. He has no children, yet."

"I left Suffrom because I wanted nothing to do with the God that the rest of my family loved. When the people on the far outreaches of Adven found me and kept me alive, I thanked them by renewing my faith in God. I became their king and I never looked back to the life I had." He took a step closer to Eli. His intensity was shown by the fire in his eyes. "Now I must. I know very little about Katherine's life, and she knows very little about my own. That must change. I love her."

"She doesn't know that you are the prince of Suffrom?"

"No one knows except you. I only told you because you've obviously been examining my bloodline." His hand swept the papers thrown all over the room. "I love Katherine. She has accepted me. I simply hope you will too."

He turned around and walked out, leaving Eli in the empty darkness of his room, alone.

Katherine sat up when she heard the knock on her door. She wiped her hand across her eyes to brush away the tears as Michael walked in. He sat down on the bed beside her.

"Everyone's settled. The gateman was very helpful." Michael laughed. "He warned me not to worry about Eli. Said he really is very happy to see us." He waited to see her reaction. She sniffed. "Adam and Edwin are making sure the rest of the men receive weapons and a good meal. Are you okay?"

She sniffed and then nodded. "This was my room, before…before I left. I grew up here. I had no idea it would turn out this way." She got up off the bed and opened the window. The crisp fall wind dropped the temperature immediately. Quickly, she closed the window again.

Michael watched her as she moved around the room, touching hairbrushes and ribbons, trailing her hand across tables and chairs, and fondling old letters and memoirs. Her mind was far away as she relived her childhood. She beckoned to him as she felt along the far wall. He quickly got up and went to her side, following her lead and feeling along the wall. Suddenly, her hand went through a small gap. Katherine pulled hard to open the secret door, then grabbed Michael's hand and pulled him in.

"This is my prayer room, mine and Ralyn's. Our mother told us about God, told Father too." She sat on the cushions along the wall. "He wouldn't listen. We prayed for him day after day after day. But, he never listened." She swiped at her eyes. The tears had returned. Michael sat down beside her. He didn't say anything, just listened. "Then Ralyn married and Father went off to war and it was just me…

just me and Eli. He really did raise me after my mother died. I didn't realize how much he cared..."

Michael took her hand as she cried. "Where is your sister now?"

"In Suffrom, with a baby on the way. She'll be giving birth soon."

"Does she know about your father?"

"I'm sure Eli told her. I left the moment I heard. I didn't stay to see what happened. Her husband's a good man; Evan will take care of her."

Michael choked. "Evan? Evan who?"

"King Evan. He took over when his father died. It was probably after you left Suffrom. Michael, are you alright?"

He stood up and paced the interior of the room. Tears filled his eyes and he covered his face with his hands. Katherine rushed to him. "Michael, what's wrong? Is it something I said? I didn't mean to burden you with my problems..." Her stomach rolled. "It's just...I hadn't mentioned my family, not really. I felt you should know. We are married after all..."

"Katherine, I should have told you...should have told you..."

"Told me what?"

He straightened. His body was still weak from the abuse he'd taken while in captivity. It took him a moment to recover and breathe normally. "I talked to Eli."

"When?"

"Before I came in here to be with you. I assured him that I loved you and that I was not a wandering vagrant."

"He didn't mean any of that. Eli was just confused..." she soothed.

"It doesn't matter, because I'm not. I'm a king of my people...but I was something before that."

"You mean, back in Suffrom?" Her eyes were shocked and confused. What did any of this mean? Would it change her and Michael...and the little one inside her? Her stomach rumbled.

"Yes." He turned to face her. "Katherine, I know Evan...King Evan. We grew up together. Do you understand?"

"Michael, if there's something you want to say just say it. I can't play these silly guessing games."

"Evan's my brother, Katherine. That's why I knew none of Eli's accusations were right. I am of *high royal blood*. I'm Prince of Suffrom. That's my title."

"Evan's your brother?"

He nodded.

Katherine just looked at him. He wasn't sure what else to say or do. They just waited.

Suddenly she laughed. A joyous ringing laugh that filled the whole castle with her happiness. "Michael! You're Evan's brother! I love you!" She threw her arms around him and danced around the room. "Praise God! I feel like I can fly!"

With that she raced from the room. Michael was left standing alone in the prayer room, a little unsure of what had just happened.

"Eli!" Katherine came bursting into the dark room, shouting his name. She slipped on one of the documents lying on the floor and fell. Laughter was heard coming from the far side of the room.

"Still a little girl at heart, Katherine?" Eli stood and shuffled his feet through the papers. When he reached her, he helped her stand.

"Michael told me everything. I'm so happy, Eli!" She grabbed his hands, but felt nothing but cold skin. "Eli?"

He sighed and sat down on the bed.

"Eli? You can't still be unsure? Eli, I love him."

Another sigh.

"Eli? Please don't be mad at me. Please talk to me; just like you used to when I *was* a little girl."

"I just want to make sure you aren't making a mistake. Are you really happy?"

"Yes, Eli."

Sad sigh. "Then I have nothing else to say." Pause. "There's something else you haven't told me." A long pause. "What is your God like?"

"My God?"

"I prayed to Him. I thought He might bring you back to me sooner."

"You prayed to Him?"

Eli nodded.

"But, how..."

"I found your prayer room. I read your proclamation. I prayed. That is it."

"You want to know about Him?"

"You seem so sure of your faith. Michael as well. I want to know why you are so sure. I prayed and offered sacrifices to the gods everyday, but felt no comfort. When I prayed to your God, I was still unsure; but I felt some comfort, like someone actually heard me."

Katherine thought for a long time. Her own faith had been so rocky of late... "Eli, the gods that you serve are weak and powerless. They cannot answer prayers and cannot grant miracles. They require much for so little. My God hears and answers your prayers. He gives miracles, like bringing me home safely. And best of all, He requires nothing. He takes you as you are without regret." She rose and walked through the mass chaos of papers to the covered windows. She tore down the drapes and light filled the room. "When He comes into your life, it is like light breaking through the darkness. And He loves you, Eli. Not just me or Ralyn. He loves you for who you are."

Eli sat on the bed surrounded by the musty papers and documents of his forefathers staring at the light shining into his formerly dark room. He felt as though he was seeing everything anew. "He is light in the darkness. I want to know that light, Katherine. I do know that light." He stood and walked to the window as he grew more passionate. "I knew from the moment I first spoke to Him that something was different. I felt that light. I know the Light." He turned to Katherine. "I will never pray to the gods again. I will pray to the God of Light."

She hugged him as tears once again streamed down her face.

Chapter Eleven

The first month went by quickly with little action. Winter came trickling in with enough snow to discourage fighting; but not enough to slow activity around the castle. When Katherine returned, life in the castle was revitalized. People laughed and talked to each other again. They had fun and did their work well. Katherine began talking with the Regents about taking over rule of the kingdom, both her and Michael. Adam, Edwin, and the other men made friends among the various people staying at the castle for the winter. The people grew to love Katherine's friends and grew to trust Michael as a future king. Winter would one day come in force; but for now, the castle was filled with warmth and laughter.

"Are you excited?"
"I'm a little nervous."
"Don't worry. Tomorrow will go exactly as planned."
Katherine rolled over to face him. "Michael, have you ever spoken to a roomful of grumpy old men who still view you as a child?"
"Yes. Not recently though." He smiled.
The single candle on the table next to the bed lit up the large bed that filled a good portion of the bedroom. Katherine and Michael had decided not to take her father and mother's old room; so, until their new room was built they were staying in a very small room used

for visiting guests. The windows were closed and covered with dark forest green drapes, but when they were open, the forest behind the castle was in full view. Other than the bed and the table, there was very little furniture. A chair sat over by the window, and a wardrobe was off to one side. The door was now closed to the outside; both because it was night, and because it kept some warmth in the room. Layer after layer of blankets lay on top of the couple, almost so they couldn't see each other, due to the fact that winter temperatures were finally here. The wind howled outside as a reminder of the current blizzard that had lasted almost a week.

"I'm nervous, Michael. What if they don't listen to me? Some of them like their status that comes from being a Regent. They don't like change; and after two and a half years, they feel almost like kings themselves."

"What can I do to help?"

She frowned. "Nothing, I suppose. You aren't allowed in the meeting; not yet anyway."

"Then there is only one person who can help."

"God?"

Michael smiled. "I'm too predictable."

"You're never predictable." She leaned over and kissed him on the cheek.

"I think it's you who are unpredictable."

Her stomach rolled. "Perhaps we should go to bed. I have a few more things to prepare tomorrow."

Michael turned over and blew out the candle.

"Princess Katherine, it is our job to interview you to make certain you are prepared for royal appointment. You are still young and newly married…"

"To a man none of us know," added another Regent.

"To a man who must also be evaluated before royal appointment," the Chief Regent glared at the offending Regent. "We have heard various testimonies both from the King's staff and others who know you. None of it gives any reason to dismiss your claim to the throne."

A younger Regent spoke up, running his hand through his graying hair. "But, there is still the matter of your youth. You are only twenty-one, and that is just barely an adult. Why should we allow you to rule the kingdom of Adven? Why shouldn't we insist you grow in your relationship with your husband and raise a family?"

Katherine stood to her feet. Her hands were shaking so she hid them behind her back. It took every ounce of concentration to keep her voice from wavering. The Regents were all looking at her. She looked every inch the Queen of Adven. She had no crown, but her confident stance told the story. Her blood was truly that of royalty, born to live and die as a Queen.

She took a few steps toward the group. It was deadly silent. Her long black dress was thick and warm, almost too warm. Finally, she spoke.

"I cannot tell you to vote one way or the other. I cannot tell you how to think or act. I can only tell you what I think. I love Adven. It is my home and my life. I have endured terrible things to make it back here safely to do what is right. My father was a great king and he did many great things for this kingdom. He died defending Adven, because he felt that was right. I have come home, because I felt that was right. Now, I am petitioning for another right. Mine. It is my right to inherit the kingdom my father left behind. As for my youth, there is no question that I am young. But that gives me all the more time to grow and learn with this kingdom. And as I grow older and more experienced, I will have more responsibility, but for now, being a queen is quite enough."

Laughter around the table.

"But what is this we hear from Eli? What about this new God?" It was the oldest and cruelest member of the Regents, the one who had made fun of her marriage. "Would you abandon the gods of our forefathers, of your father, and follow a new untested God?"

"He is far from untested, as Eli will testify to, if asked. He has stood the test of time and of many doubts and questions, from me and the others who follow Him. Michael…"

"See! Her husband has led her astray! He has convinced her to follow a false god and turn away from the true ones!"

The council erupted in commotion. The various Regents were shouting and fighting; the Chief Regent was trying to regain control. Her chance at the kingdom would be lost if it didn't stop.

Katherine leapt on top of the table that had been placed in the center of the room. Papers and notes scattered and there was more shouting and confusion. She drew her sword and the light that flashed from it brought instant calm. With the sword in her hand pointed at the sky, she spoke.

"Who here would deface the name of Queen Aimi?"

No one said a word.

"It was not Michael who led me to God. It was my mother, Queen Aimi."

"Lies!" shouted the ancient Regent.

"Truth! Do you want the truth? The truth is my mother Aimi brought love and life into my life. When she died, had it not been for my faith, I would have died with her. She also brought Ralyn to believe in Him. He is true. Whether you believe me or not, believe that Queen Aimi would not have led me astray. She would not have led anyone astray."

The ancient Regent was furious. "You think you can become queen by coming in here, giving a speech and waving a sword. We are civilized, and you have proven what a child you are! I call for the vote now!"

"I second it!" cried someone else.

The Chief Regent waved his hand and said, "She is not allowed in here for the vote!"

"I vote nay!" the ancient Regent cried. "Who votes with me?"

"I am still Chief Regent and there are still rules to follow! Princess Katherine must either continue her questioning or leave for the vote."

"She must leave!" The ancient Regent pointed an accusing finger at her. "I know all I need to know! She is unfit to be queen!"

Katherine let her anger get the best of her. "And you are unfit to be a Regent!"

"Princess Katherine!"

Her sword had come dangerously close to the offending Regent's head. She sheathed it and marched out, listening as the argument continued behind her.

"Katherine, it's not your fault. There was nothing you could do."

Her pacing was violent. Ignoring Michael's pleas to eat while she waited, she had done nothing but pace for the last two hours. The argument still continued. The Regents could not decide what to do about her. The council was divided between the ancient Regent who voted against her and the younger Regent who voted with her. The Chief Regent was having a terrible time keeping order, because tempers were so high.

"There was nothing you could do."

"They accused you of leading me away from the gods! I couldn't let that stand. I knew there was no way they'd accuse my mother. They adore Queen Aimi."

"Katherine, just calm down."

She glared at him. "I will not calm down! A group of old big mouths are the only thing standing between me and the kingdom of Adven. While they sit in their council chamber, there is a madman out there trying to destroy me!"

Her fist pounded the table. The sound echoed throughout the great hall, where she and Michael were at one end of the long table. The servants kept the huge fireplace going constantly, in an attempt to keep the castle warm. The fire flickered and danced on the metal of Katherine's sword, which sat on the table after Michael insisted she best not carry it while she paced.

Footsteps echoed across the tile floor as Adam and Edwin entered. Adam spoke first. "We heard what happened. Your stable boys are rather chatty. When we didn't hear anything else, we felt it wise to see how you were."

Edwin chuckled. "It didn't take long to find you. The servants are all scared to come in and stoke the fire."

Her shoulders fell. "I didn't mean to upset anybody. Those silly Regents just…"

Michael eased her into a chair. He stroked his beard while he thought about what to say. The other men took chairs next to Katherine and him.

Katherine felt sick. Her stomach rumbled. It was a miracle she had not lost this baby. She had heard horror stories like that, where women lost their children because they were upset or traumatized. Why was God going to such lengths to keep this one alive?

"Katherine?"

She raised her head and tried to focus sleepy eyes. "Michael?"

"No. It's Eli. Michael came and found me; he thought maybe I could convince you to go to sleep." He sat down at the table beside her.

"I have to wait and see what the Regents say."

He shook his head. "You know them. They'll argue halfway through the night before they realize the sun went down. They're not going anywhere, remember? There's still a blizzard going on."

"Is everyone safely inside?"

"Yes. I've checked on everyone."

"Have you heard anything from Ralyn?"

"No. Were you expecting something?"

Katherine nodded. "Wasn't her baby due some time ago?"

Eli laughed and helped her stand. "I'm sure all is well and Olvin is on his way to tell us the good news. Now, you should go to bed. I'll come and get you if the Regents decide anything. Michael is worried about you."

She hugged him. "I'm glad the two of you are getting along now."

"I didn't have much of a choice, did I?"

Katherine crawled into bed beside Michael, who appeared to be asleep. It was dark and cold when she finally got comfortable and closed her eyes. It seemed like only a minute before someone was shaking her awake.

"Katherine! Katherine! Katherine!"

"Huh? Who? What?"

"Katherine! The council has called Michael to testify."

Finally, she awoke. Eli was frantically shaking her and shouting to get her to understand. "He's in there now, Katherine! Do you understand?"

"Where is Michael?"

"He's in the council with the Regents. They are questioning him to approve him for royal appointment!"

She leaped out of bed and began to throw her clothes on. "Why didn't you say that?" And she rushed out of the room.

Adam and Edwin were standing guard at the door to the Council Room. It was clear they weren't sure what to think or do. Katherine came running up to them and immediately peppered them with questions.

"How long has he been in there?"

"About half an hour."

"What did they say when they called for him?"

"I don't know."

"Why didn't anyone wake me sooner?"

"Michael said to let you sleep. He didn't want you to worry."

"Do you know what's going on?"

"Not at all."

"Adam, you must know something!"

He turned to Edwin, who shrugged. "I've told you all I know."

Frustrated, she sat on the ground.

Chapter Twelve

"Michael, you must understand our hesitancy. We know nothing about you, your family, or where you come from." The Chief Regent sat at the head of the table with his hands folded together on the table in front of him. The other Regents were watching anxiously Michael's every move. Some had seemed to warm to him immediately; they had conversed with him as they wandered around the castle. Others, like the old Regent so determined to vote Katherine down, were skeptical. Here was a man, practically a boy, who came from nowhere and whom they knew nothing about. "Of course," the Chief Regent continued, "we have heard Eli's testimony and the lineage you claim. With this current blizzard, there is no way we can get through to Suffrom and confirm your story. What else can you offer to our table?"

Michael had been waiting patiently at the end of the table for his turn to speak. He had not moved since the servant had announced him and ushered him to his place. His eyes were warm and thoughtful, filled with wisdom. In fact, he looked very much like Katherine looked, in all her fiery anger. He looked every inch the King of Adven.

"There is nothing that I can say to change the minds of some." Many eyes turned to the ancient Regent; who scowled at Michael in return. "Others of you are already decided in my favor." The youngest Regent, who eagerly supported Katherine, smiled a pleased smile at the recognition. "It is those who are undecided to whom I speak.

It is your minds I wish to challenge." The Chief Regent cocked an eyebrow. Michael paused a moment before continuing. His voice was calm and even, but filled with emotion.

"Let us suppose that I have lied. For imagination's sake, let us say that I didn't grow up in Suffrom, my father was not the king, and my brother is not King Evan, the husband of Katherine's sister. Instead, let me be a commoner who grew up on the outskirts of Adven. My parents were normal parents who tried to give me an education, but couldn't. I was an only child and the pride of my family. Let us suppose that this is my story."

The ancient Regent pointed a questioning finger at Michael, "You weave this supposedly false story very well. Too well in fact. How do we know that this is not the truth?"

"My renown as a storyteller is well-known. Ask any of my men. It is one of the qualities that drew me as an orphan to be so well-liked by their community. The stories I tell may or may not be true but they have meaning, something many people lack when they speak."

The Regents were silent at the young man's wisdom. How could he not have been trained as a Prince if he speaks so well?

"Back to the story of our imaginations. You have a poor boy that somehow happened upon a community willing enough to take him in. He grew to become the leader of this community. One day a princess is rescued by this poor boy and they are married. Would you look at that?" He paused. "The story has the same result. A man's upbringing doesn't affect his courage or his character. In fact, many princes I have known lack both of these princely qualities. But, I have also known many paupers more courageous that one could imagine." Here he pointed to the door where he knew Adam and Edwin were waiting. "There are two fine examples just beyond this door. What makes a man is not his upbringing, but his faith."

Again an interruption from the ancient Regent. "Here comes the blasphemy. How can you defend your belief in a false God?"

Michael quietly repeated the questioned and redirected it, "How can you defend your belief in a false god?"

Chaos erupted for a moment. The question of God was a question the Chief Regent had hoped to ignore. Secretly, he hoped the Council would hear no more of it. However, the question could not be avoided now. "Please, Michael, explain yourself. The traditions here in Adven have been held for centuries. You cannot expect to change all of our minds in one day."

"But, that is where you are wrong. My God is powerful enough to change the hearts of all men, all in one moment if He chose. Which one of you will make that claim of your gods?"

No one could raise their hands. They had all been disappointed in their worship more than once. Sometimes the gods simply didn't hear their prayers. But, that was expected…wasn't it?

"There is a God who hears your prayers. There is a God who answers your questions. There is a God who cares about you problems. There is a God who loves you; if you will let Him."

All was silent in the room. Every Regent hung on Michael's words. They had heard little bits from Eli and Katherine. Most had never spoken directly to Michael about his faith in his God. Now he was explaining in almost painful plainness that the God he believed in was real.

"The testimonies of Eli, Katherine, Adam, Edwin, and myself should be enough to convince you, but if they are not, test God Himself. He will not shrink from it, nor will He hide. Your prayers will be answered, but do not always expect a yes. God is perfect, but we are not. Sometimes our prayers are not what is best; they are often quite selfish. But God loves you. He wants the best for you and will answer what is best. Will you let Him? Will you listen to what He has to say?"

For a moment, no one moved. The air was heavy with anticipation. Not a breath was heard from anyone. Then, the youngest Regent stood. His hands held the table to keep himself steady and tears streamed down his face.

"I do not need any proof," he said shakily. "What must I do to call on His name? What must I do to make Him my God?"

Another minute of silence as Michael waited. The young Regent fidgeted, waiting for a reply to his questions. Still, Michael waited.

When the young Regent was about to speak again, Michael put up his hand. At that moment the Chief Regent stood to his feet.

"I need no convincing either. What must I do to know your God?"

Michael still said nothing but waited for another half a second. Then as one, the rest of the table rose, all but one. The ancient Regent still sat in his chair.

In that moment, all the rest asked the same question in various ways. "How do I know Him?" Still, Michael waited.

The last Regent stood. He looked Michael straight in the face. "Today you have proven your God exists." His hand swept the room. "Today your God has moved the hearts of all the Regents. Who am I to question His existence?"

A knock on the big wooden doors startled Katherine. Adam, Edwin, Eli, and herself had sat waiting at the door for longer than she felt was comfortable. In fact, she had just thought about standing to stretch when the knock came. Quickly, the four scrambled out of the way of the door as it opened out. They stood looking at each other confused when not Michael, but the youngest Regent stood looking at them from the open doorway. His hair was mussed and there were tear stains on his cheeks, but his face showed no other emotion.

"The Council is requesting your presence, Princess Katherine."

"Right now?"

He nodded.

"Is Michael in there?"

"Your husband is waiting for you."

"Give me just a moment."

The Regent nodded and walked back into the room. The door gently closed behind him.

Katherine looked at the astonished faces of her friends. "What do you make of that?"

"Perhaps you better go in quickly," Eli said. "The Regents won't keep waiting long."

Adam and Edwin both nodded at the wise suggestion.

She straightened her clothes, placed her hand on her sword hilt, opened the door, and walked into the Council Room.

The room was deathly quiet. All of the Regents stood at their places when she entered. Michael was still standing in his place at the foot of the table. Every eye was on Katherine as she walked to stand by her husband. When she was situated, the Regents sat.

"Princess Katherine, we have reached a decision. It might interest you to know that we forsook the oldest rules and customs and voted with your husband present. It was a unanimous vote and there was no need for secrecy. Would the two of you please stand before the Council?"

Michael reached for her hand and led her to stand before the Chief Regent at the head of the table. Again, all eyes were on her. Her stomach fluttered and she felt sick. All of her life had been spent preparing for this moment; and now it had come, fast and furious.

"Your Majesties, the Council has voted on the matter of bestowing kingship upon Prince Michael of Suffrom, son of Benjamin, former King of Suffrom and brother of Evan, King of Suffrom. Also, on the matter of bestowing queenship to the heir of Adven, Princess Katherine, daughter of Andrew, former King of Adven and sister of Ralyn, Queen of Suffrom." Here he paused to take a breath. These types of occasions were very long and wordy, due to the formality. "The Regent of records will now read the vote."

The ancient Regent, the Regent of records, stood to his feet. His voice spoke evenly and sternly. "The Council of Adven voted this day on the matter of kingship and queenship being bestowed upon those aforementioned. The vote was as follows: all members of the Council of Adven, the Regents of this country in the absence of King Andrew voted unanimously." He paused and watched Katherine. She waited anxiously clutching Michael's hand. At the last moment, a smile flickered through his eyes. "To approve the bestowal of said kingship and queenship on those aforementioned."

Katherine let out a gasp and tears of joy rippled down her cheeks. She collapsed to the floor and cried, her loud sobs echoing across the Council chamber. Michael continued to hold her hand as she cried.

After a moment, he whispered in her ear, "Perhaps you should stand again. They aren't finished."

Her quick glance at his excited face calmed her tears. Quickly, she stood to her feet once more, brushing the tears from her cheeks.

The Chief Regent smiled at her fussing. His reassurance quieted any fears still lingering. "The Council must also announce a decision, also unanimous, made this day…"

The young Regent could wait no more. He leapt to his feet without waiting for his name to be called. "We have come to know your God, Queen Katherine! He is our God too…all of us." The smiles on every face confirmed the story.

Her tears began anew as she rushed about, hugging every Regent from the oldest to the youngest. "I have never heard such good news! I'm so happy for all of you!" And without waiting for a response, she threw open the chamber doors.

"Eli! Adam! Edwin! Come and hear what the Council has to say!"

The date for the coronation was set for three months from that day. Winter would be coming to a close, but there would hopefully be no enemy present yet. Preparations began right away, as it would be a grand affair. Every day Katherine spent hours cleaning, organizing, and running errands around the castle. Adam had appointed himself chief instructor of the knights and had them constantly running drills when they were not pressed into the service of Katherine's cleaning crew. Edwin used most of his time working with the horses in the stable. Even though his family was poor, they had owned a few horses and they had been his pride and joy. Now, that the opportunity to work with them was given again; and he took every advantage of it. Michael was often found reading Queen Aimi's vast library. While King Andrew had not been a lover of books, his wife was; and so she owned many books of history and kingly duties. The future king was constantly studying and renewing his past lessons of kingship. Eli also exhausted his time studying. But, he was not studying kings; he was studying gods. His God was not mentioned in Adven's history and he wanted to know why.

Chapter Thirteen

"Michael? Are you in here?"

Katherine gently nudged the door open with her foot. With a quiet creak, the heavy wooden door swung open a crack. Readjusting the tray which she carried, she put more weight against the door. Finally, it opened enough for her to squeeze in. The clinking of the plates and silverware sounded loud and abrasive in her ears compared to the quiet calm of her mother's library.

Many hours of her childhood had been spent in this very room. As the eldest child, she was expected to learn not only the ways of war and of kingship, but of literature and of learning. Many afternoons she would come running from her sword lessons with her father into the library. Her mother always stood sternly behind the desk where she kept her teaching supplies, waiting for her to arrive. Katherine had often come later than expected and her tardiness didn't go unnoticed.

"Katherine," her mother would say. "You're a princess. Princesses aren't tardy." This was usually followed by a visual inspection of her torn dress, dirty shoes, and tangled hair. "And they don't come to their lessons looking like a peasant."

Princess Katherine would then hang her head in shame. She knew what was expected, but how was she to be on time as well as clean?

Then Queen Aimi would smile. "But you are my princess and I love you, just the way you are. Just the way God loves you."

Then Katherine would study harder and learn faster. She really had been quite a brilliant student both in her studies and her swordsmanship. Ralyn was too timid to handle a sword and too shy to read aloud. But Katherine? She relished in excelling in everything. But sometimes, when she was concentrating very hard, her mind would wander and her mother would have to call her attention back to her studies...

"Katherine?"

With a jerk, Katherine returned out of her reminiscing. Michael was looking up at her, waiting patiently for an answer. His eyes looked tired but excited. Joy and contentment were in them because he was doing what he was born to do. His hands rested on the many scrolls and books spread before him on Queen Aimi's desk.

"I brought you something to eat. We missed you at dinner."

He gratefully accepted the tray and cleared a place for it on the desk. "Thank you, I was so engrossed I didn't even notice how late it was." When she had set the tray down, he motioned her to come and read over his shoulder. She leaned over him, holding her hair in one hand so as not to be in the way of the words.

"Look, here is a list of the ancient qualities of kings. They must be noble, wise, honest, valiant, kind, just, and patient. These are all qualities that a follower of God must have!" He glanced at her with an eager expression. "Just think! Even those who are without God seek those who know Him! Why, one practically must be a follower of the true God to meet all these qualities. Now of course, we aren't perfect either. We get angry and impatient. We can be mean and cruel to those we love most. We hide things that ought to be told..."

As he continued speaking, Katherine's mind wandered. *We hide things that ought to be told...* It was almost as though he could read her thoughts. Every day she felt the baby growing inside her and the secret growing harder to keep. Her height helped her. Because she was taller than most, the baby grew up instead of out, allowing her to little by little let out the seams of her dresses and no one notice the slight change. But, really, she shouldn't be afraid to tell. There is nothing wrong! The baby will be due in...what was it now? Five months. The baby was four months old; and therefore it would be born in five months. So much could happen in five months. In less than two months would be the coronation and soon after that the war would begin again. She would be six, almost seven, months pregnant by that time! She would have to tell Michael. What better time than now? Here in the safety of her mother's library she could tell him everything.

"Isn't that fascinating?"

Her mind searched for what he'd just been speaking of, but could come up with nothing.

Michael sighed softly. "I suppose it is only interesting to me. I'm boring you. Was there any other thing you needed to tell me?"

"Yes."

He waited for her to tell.

"I just wanted to tell you..." she faltered. His eyes were so beautiful. Would their baby have eyes like his? So brown, so knowledgeable, so soft and sweet...

"Yes? Is something wrong?"

The alarm in his voice disrupted her thoughts. "No! Nothing at all is wrong...I just wanted to tell you..." She took a deep breath and continued. "I love you."

He breathed a sigh of relief. "Is that all?" His arms reached out and pulled her close. With his hands clasped around her waist he pulled her face close to his. "I love you too. My love conquers all things, even death, just like God's love does for you."

It was so similar to her mother's gentle reassurance of love that Katherine found it hard to distinguish memories from present. Michael's eyes were so full of that love, that deep unending love, just like her mother's. It pained her to keep the baby from him, but now was not the time. Not that she wouldn't tell him. She just wouldn't tell him now.

"I'll leave you to your studies." She gently untwined his fingers and moved away. Before she walked completely away she turned to face him once more. There he sat in her mother's chair, face full of love for her. Quietly, she kissed him on the forehead before turning toward the door. After she'd pulled it shut behind her, Michael sighed.

KATHERINE'S KINGDOM: TO LOVE IN PEACE

"I love you, Queen Katherine. What are you keeping from me?"

The quiet neighs of horses and the sweet smell of straw accompanied the creak of the stable door as Katherine opened it. All the various shades of color seemed to be represented here in this one room. The reds, browns, tans, grays, blacks, and whites covered every flank and mane. Noses pressed into her hands as she walked past the stalls, each begging for a treat with their gently nudging.

As she reached the last stall, she smiled and held in a laugh. Edwin stood mucking out the stall with his large shovel. Every inch of him was covered in mud, straw, and other unrecognizable things. You could barely see the freckles across his nose. His red hair was plastered to his face with sweat and he wiped one mud covered hand across his pale brow. Even the little bit of red stubble he called a beard was clogged with muck.

Her smothered laugh startled him and he glanced up. Quickly his face went from pale to bright red. "Your Majesty," he stuttered. "I…I didn't know you were here. How can I help you?"

"I need a horse Edwin. She doesn't need to be fast, I just want to go for a ride."

He glanced out the window at the falling snowflakes. "But, it's quite cold outside. Wouldn't you rather stay inside by the fire?"

"I've been sitting by the fire. I want to go out now."

"But what if you get lost? How would we find you?"

She shook her head. "I'm not going far, and besides, I grew up here remember?"

"Yes, but… what if the enemy is out there?"

"Then the watchmen have not done their jobs. Now, if there are no more questions I will go on my ride."

"But…"

Katherine came close and leaned into his muddy face, speaking in a harsh whisper. "Edwin, don't make me order you to give me a horse. Just help me out. I won't be gone long. If anything happens I'll come right back."

Reluctantly, Edwin saddled a horse for her and helped her up. He held the reins and led her to the gatehouse door. After a quick word with the gateman, the door was opened and Katherine waved goodbye while riding out into the white wilderness.

Adam was sharpening various swords when Edwin came rushing up to him. The young man looked only slightly cleaner than when he had been in the stables. In fact, the horse smell was so strong that Adam knew exactly who it was before he turned around.

"Edwin, you should really wash some of that smell off you before you enter civilization again."

"Sorry, sir, but…"

"Sir? It's Adam."

"Sorry, Adam, but…"

Finally he turned around, wiping his hands on a cloth sitting nearby. His face was full of laughter. He did enjoy twisting this young man's tongue. "Go on. Spit it out."

"Queen Katherine has left, sir."

Adam almost choked. "Left? Left where? How long ago?"

In his fear, the older man had backed Edwin up against the wall. "Please, Adam, I told her not to go. But, she wouldn't listen!"

Adam's strong fist grabbed Edwin's collar. "Where did she go and how long ago did she leave?"

"She went for a ride outside the castle walls and she left about an hour ago. I waited for her to return, she said she wouldn't go far or be long, but then the snow grew worse…"

"Enough! Get me my horse! Run, Edwin!"

The young man was out the door before Adam could finish his thought.

Michael stood stiffly. He stretched his limbs and looked out the window. The snowflakes danced lightly across the panes and floated to the ground. It looked like there was another blizzard in the making. In the courtyard below him, men were wandering to and fro. Some looked like there was no purpose to their steps; others looked as if their life depended on the errand they were running. He could see Adam gesturing and Edwin running back and forth from the stable. The snow obscured his vision, but it looked as though a crowd was gathering. Was Adam thinking of running drills in this blizzard?

He shook his head. He would go down and see what the fuss was about. No one needed to be out and about in a blizzard like this.

"Men, come quickly! We know her majesty has been out for about an hour. She shouldn't have gone far from the castle, but with this blizzard we can't be sure of that. Go out in groups of three and do not get separated! Our only task is to find the Queen before something happens to her! Now…"

At that moment the gate clanged open. Katherine's horse trotted in among the others gathered in the courtyard. About twenty men were standing staring at their queen. She looked at the group before her. Her eyes fell on Edwin who slipped behind Adam. Adam's eyes were searching her, evaluating her every movement.

"What's going on?"

Adam dismounted and walked toward her. "You were gone for a long time. We were worried about you."

"I can take care of myself." She also dismounted and handed her reins to Edwin, eager to help.

"What were you doing?" Adam stepped closer to her as they spoke. His eyes were cold and searching.

"Going for a ride. I wanted outside the castle walls." She started to leave, but Adam grasped her arm.

"You weren't running away again?"

Her face blushed. That was exactly what she had intended, but decided against it. She was Queen. There was no escaping that fact now, no matter how much she wished otherwise. "How dare you." Her anger seeped into every word. She was furious that Adam would suspect her of something so cowardly, even if it was true. "How dare you accuse me of deserting. How dare you!"

Adam looked her straight in the eye. He knew exactly what was going on.

"You think I can't take care of myself? That I'm not in control? That I don't know exactly what's going on?" Her fury rose to a higher pitch. "How dare you!" She turned on Edwin. "And I suppose you were party to this?" Before he could answer, her eyes were drawn elsewhere.

Michael had just walked down the stairs and come out into the courtyard. There was a smile on his face as he saw Katherine, Adam, and Edwin talking. She was probably telling them what he was going to say, that no one should be outside in a blizzard like this. He was surprised to see her glare at him in anger. He stopped about ten feet from her, confusion clear on his face.

"You probably started it! You told them I couldn't be trusted! How dare you!" Her accusing finger carried her right to Michael's face. Her heart told her she was making a mistake, but she was too angry to care. Her stomach grumbled at her.

"Katherine, what are you talking about?"

Furious, she shoved past him and marched up the stairs.

Michael turned to the sheepish men standing before him. Adam's eyes were still following Katherine as she walked up the stairs, and Edwin had just come out from behind the older man.

"Would someone like to explain what just happened?"

Katherine flung herself on her bed. She felt sick and disgusted with herself. How could she lead anyone? She couldn't even keep herself under control! Every word that had just come out of her mouth was a lie, and she knew it. Adam and Edwin and all the rest had only been trying to help her. They were concerned. She wasn't sure where Michael fell into the mess, but she suspected he truly had no idea what just happened.

Anger was quickly turning into remorse and embarrassment. She knew she owed everyone an apology. That much was certain. A sigh escaped her lips. What was happening to her? Her whole life had been training for leadership. Why was she running now that her destiny had finally arrived?

Her stomach rumbled and she felt sick. She knew why she wanted to run. All of the training in the world couldn't have prepared her for being a mother. This baby was something totally unexpected and frightening. Katherine would rather fight a thousand men than be responsible for the life of the baby inside of her. How did she even know she could take care of him…or her? What would Michael say when he found out? What if he didn't want children? It wasn't really something they'd talked about. Another sigh.

"What am I going to do?"

"About what?"

Michael poked his head in the bedroom door and saw his wife sprawled on the bed. Tears were slipping down her cheeks and off the end of her nose. Even with her hair tussled and her dress wrinkled, she was beautiful to him. Every part of her was something to love and cherish, even the tears. He sat on the edge of the bed and waited while she readjusted to make room for him.

She sighed once again. "Nothing. Well…something." Could she tell him now? Certainly not after the way she'd treated him.

"You know you can tell me anything. What's wrong?" His eyes were waiting patiently for the truth, and not just part of it. He wanted everything.

Katherine wanted to. She wanted to tell him how scared she was. She wanted to share the burden of her secret. But, it had been four months now that she had hidden the truth. She couldn't blurt it all out in one moment.

"I'm just so embarrassed by the way I acted. I shouldn't have spoken that way to anyone, especially you."

"It's already forgiven."

His kind smile reassured her to continue pouring out her feelings. "I'm so confused right now. I have so many questions."

"Like what?"

"Like…why is there a madman chasing me and wanting to ruin Adven?"

"He wants to get back at your father. He resents the position you hold."

"But why me?"

"Because your father is dead. You and your sister were the closest thing to him. Ralyn is in Suffrom. You are easier to torment."

His ready answers frustrated her. It made it sound like common knowledge, but it truly didn't make sense to her. "Why did my father have to die?"

"I don't know."

She looked at him puzzled. Michael smiled his easygoing smile. "I'm not God. I don't know everything."

Her eyes searched the room for another question to help explain her emotions. They landed on her sword leaning on the wall opposite her. Now it looked dull and hidden by the shadows, but her mind still saw it glistening as she raised it against her enemies.

She stood to her feet, walked over and picked up the sword. It felt heavy in her hands, like she'd picked up the burden of her secret instead of picking up the sword in its sheath. "What about this?"

"What about it?"

"Why did it do what it did?"

"What do you mean?"

His gentle probing frustrated her. "The way it blinded those men coming after us. It looked like lightning in the sky. I didn't even have to do anything! It just…" The question trailed off into silence as she lost the words to complete the thought.

"I don't know that answer either."

He got off the bed and walked to her. He took the sword from her hand and looked at it. The sheath was hard leather and a dull brown. The hilt gave a tiny hint as to the well-made sword attached to it, hiding in the sheath. "Sometimes God wants things to remain a mystery. It reminds us of the miracles He provides and the help He gives." He returned the sword to her, letting it drop lightly into her waiting hands. "As for the questions, He can answer those as well. Ask Him, not me, and you may get better answers."

She nodded. Her heart pondered all her husband had said.

"Katherine?"

"Hm?"

"May I ask you a question?"

"Yes."

He reached over and led her to the bed. The sword sat in her lap with her hands settled on top of it. Michael's hand gently reached over to cover his wife's. "What are you hiding from me?"

Emotion leapt into her throat. This was her chance! She could tell him everything. About the baby. About her fears of being an inadequate mother. About her fears he'd be worried about her.

Her mouth opened to tell him, but her mind reminded her of the letter Ralyn had sent all those months ago. *The doctor has had to tell King Evan a thousand times to let me be. If he had his way I would never leave my chambers.*

The thought invaded her mind, filling it with pictures of being forced to stay in her room, to stop her duties around the castle, to stay behind when the war started again…

She shook her head. Michael would be too loving. He would be just like Evan, wanting her to stay put and not move. She'd taken care of this baby for four months and nothing had happened yet! Nothing would ever happen to this baby.

"I'm not hiding anything." She smiled prettily at him and bobbed her head to one side. It completed the innocent look. "What made you think I was?"

Michael's eyes searched his wife's. Her smile lit up her face and her voice showed no hint of the tears streaking her face earlier. But, in her eyes there was a distance. Something like a wall separated him from seeing what she really felt. There was no doubt about it. She was hiding something. "Nothing I suppose."

Her smile widened, but it still didn't reach her eyes. Gently, she leaned over and kissed Michael on the cheek. He almost flinched, and it surprised him. The kiss wasn't full of love or affection. It was cold and empty. She was trying to distract him and set aside his fears.

Katherine leaned back and smiled again. "I'd best go apologize to those in the courtyard for my thoughtless actions." She stood and strapped her sword to her belt. It was long almost reaching her ankles. The brown leather sheath blended in with her dark green dress. The material was so dark it looked like it held a whole forest inside the weavings. As she walked to the door, it swished around her ankles and almost succeeded in distracting him from his questions. "I'll see you later, Michael."

He nodded and watched her walk out the door. When she closed it behind her, tears started to come to his eyes and he bowed his head. "God, what is she hiding from me? Why won't she trust me? I love her, but it's so hard when there's something between us."

The silence in the room met his prayer. He sighed and left to tend to his other duties before the evening meal.

Chapter Fourteen

Days flew by as preparations for the coronation continued. The incident in the courtyard was readily forgiven by all involved, and Katherine pushed aside any residual guilt or misgivings to continue her work. Everyday was another opportunity to prepare and learn and grow. She took advantage of every opportunity to do something new or different, to make a new friend or support an old friendship. The fighting emotions within her gave her the energy to keep going when everyone around her was tired of working, tired of waiting, and tired of winter.

The knights were getting the rest they needed for the long road ahead. Michael's men were learning the skills they needed to interact with the enemy in the same manner as the rest of the knights of Adven. Everyday Adam would drill them and work right alongside the other instructors to learn and grow himself, as well as teach the men. Everyone grew strong and confident, ready to battle for the kingdom they loved and the young king and queen they respected. Even the drudgery of repeated work day after day couldn't discourage their eagerness to grow and fight better.

Everyone prospered and felt comfortable during the cold winter that enveloped them. There was plenty of food and drink, plenty of wood to burn in the fire, and plenty of stories and songs to tell and to sing. In fact, everyone was satisfied except Michael. The thought that

Katherine was keeping something from him ate at his thoughts and heart. Outwardly, she showed no sign of it, but every time she brushed past him or planted a kiss on his cheek he could sense her distance. The act was good. No one else knew or even suspected. But he knew.

Time after time he would try to talk to her. They would talk about the coronation, and then the war; but when he tried to talk about after the war, about peace and prosperity, about having time to build a family of their own... She would suddenly have something to do or be called away. Always Katherine would promise to finish the conversation later, but they never did. Each night Michael would come into their bedroom hoping for a chance to talk in that precious space of time before they went to sleep, but she would already be asleep. Every night, he would pray, kiss her on the cheek, and crawl in bed beside her. And every night, his sleep would be disturbed by the fact that they hadn't really spoken in a month.

The door creaked open quietly as Michael entered the dark bedroom. His candle revealed his wife's sleeping form lying on their bed. She was covered in blankets all the way up to her ears, but her hair was lying in its braid on top of the covers. He watched her breathing cause the blanket to move up and down gently.

Carefully, he tiptoed around the bed and set down the candle. He crawled into bed and leaned over Katherine. "I love you. You know that, right? 'Place me as a seal over your heart.' I'll keep your secrets if only you'd tell them to me." With that he kissed her, breathed a silent prayer, and went to sleep.

He didn't see Katherine's tears running down her face as she opened her eyes in the darkness.

The nightmares had returned. Distorted pictures ran through her mind. Her father swinging her through the air as a child, but no! It wasn't him, it was Michael...but it wasn't her...who was that little girl? But then he let go and she went sailing through the air, but it wasn't the little girl falling...it was Katherine. She screamed as she fell to the ground, but she never felt the impact. It was the little girl lying crumpled on the ground.

"Are you alright?" The wind whipped Katherine's question away before the question reached the still form on the ground. "Someone help her! I think she's hurt!"

Katherine turned in circles repeating her call for help. When she turned to look at the still form, it was no longer a little girl, but her father! "Father! I'm sorry! I love you!" Of course, he didn't respond. He was dead. But, it wasn't her father…

"Michael! What happened?" She ran to him and shook him. He didn't respond. Katherine heard the madman's voice laughing somewhere is the mess. "Michael," she whispered. "Don't leave me alone!"

Sobbing. Weeping. Where was it coming from? The little girl! She was standing over Michael weeping. But why? "Who are you?"

The pictures dissolved into blackness pierced by insane laughter. "No! He's not dead! He's right here beside me! Michael? Michael? Where are you? God, where are you!?"

With that, Katherine shot up straight in the bed. Her clothes were drenched with sweat. Her hair was flying in all directions. Relaxing, she patted the bed to her left, expecting Michael to still be asleep beside her. But, her hand touched empty air.

"Michael?" Panic rushed through her at the thought that her husband was no longer in the bed with her. "Where are you?" Her nightmare rushed through her mind in painful clarity.

Shivering in the coldness of the dark night, she slipped from the bed. Her hand shook as it reached for the candle sitting on the table on Michael's side of the bed. It wasn't there! Frightened, she turned her attention to the dark hallway beyond the bedroom. The empty blackness looked like it would swallow her up if she stepped foot in it.

Trying to overcome her fear, she peeked around the open doorway. The sound of the night wind whistling through the empty hallways frightened her. She shivered again. Terror was grasping hold of her and threatening to send her screaming back to her bed. With the remnants of her dream whipping through her mind, Katherine stepped into the hallway.

Never before had her own castle terrified her so much. Every cough or snore sent her scurrying to one side. Her heart pounded wildly and her stomach did flip flops with every step she took. The hallway was so empty! Wasn't there anyone in the castle awake besides her? Her soft footfalls echoed off every wall, magnifying her fear.

Down the hallway, a turn to the left, descending stairs, and then...

A sound! Coming from the opposite direction! Frantically, Katherine looked for a place to hide, but all the doors were shut and locked for the night. The light of an approaching candle danced on the walls around the corner, and her heart danced in her chest.

Stop right now, Katherine! It's probably just the maid tidying up. Or that little servant girl is sleep walking. Or some sleepless knight is making his rounds...Why didn't I think to bring my sword?

With nothing to defend herself and nowhere to hide, she braced herself for the worst. Every nightmare she'd ever had flashed through her mind, and her knees shook uncontrollably. Around the corner came the light...

"Michael!" she yelled and nearly fainted.

He ran to catch her, setting the candle on the floor as he flew by. "Are you alright? What are you doing out of bed?"

Katherine's stomach flipped. Apparently, the baby didn't appreciate the excitement. Her face paled.

"Are you alright?" he repeated. Concern was etched on his face.

"I'm alright. You scared me. What were *you* doing out of bed?"

"I couldn't sleep and I went for a walk. Are you sure everything's alright?"

She wrenched out of his grasp. "Of course I'm alright! Now that I'm sure my husband is safe and sound, I'm going back to bed." And with that, Katherine, Princess of Adven, turned around and marched back to her bedroom.

Michael shook his head and quietly followed her back to bed, picking up the candle as he went.

The morning light couldn't pierce Katherine's dark mood. Her nightmare had frightened her terribly, more than she wanted to admit. As she dressed and began to move about her day, the darkness hung on her like a thick cloak.

"Katherine?"

She turned to look at her husband. The concern she had seen on Michael's face the night before was still there. It filled her heart with the pain of her nightmares and the burdens of her secrets, but what could she do? Tangled in the lies she had woven, there was nothing to do but continue the charade. "I'm fine, Michael. Would you please stop asking?"

The concern is his eyes changed to pain as she shut him out. But, she had no choice. That was what she had to keep telling herself. Turning her attention to the papers before her, she continued. "What is the status of the training?"

Michael cleared his throat before answering. "Everything is moving faster than we planned. Actually, Adam wanted us to inspect the knights this afternoon."

"Assuming it stops snowing?"

He laughed. "Assuming it stops snowing. Although, knowing Adam, he'd march the knights out in the snow and claim it was part of their training." He stopped laughing. "So, I'll say we're coming."

Katherine nodded as she looked over more paperwork. The papers were spread out over the table in the Hall. The couple shared the corner closest to the fireplace. Close enough for warmth, but not too warm. Hard bread left over from breakfast sat a little ways away, and Michael munched on it from time to time, chewing thoughtfully. He thought this would be a good time to try conversing again. They were alone. Surely no one would need them for awhile. Maybe this time she would talk to him.

"Katherine..."

Knock. Knock. Knock.

"Enter!" Her voice echoed across the hall. Michael's ears danced at the lilting melody. He loved her so much. There was no doubt about it.

"Your Majesties." Edwin entered and bowed. "I'm sorry to interrupt, but Princess Katherine is needed at the Council. Your presence will be required later Michael. That was the message I was to deliver." Another stiff bow and he was gone.

Katherine sighed and stretched as she stood. "We'll have to finish this later. I wonder what the Council wants."

"Probably more details about the coronation."

"Probably." She stretched again. "Are you coming?"

"I'll be along later."

"Alright." A peck on the cheek. "I promise I'm fine, Michael. Really."

Before he could object, she was out the door. The fire crackled beside him, but Michael felt cold and very much alone.

It did indeed stop snowing for the enterprising Adam. All the knights were out with swords ready to present before their future king and queen. As the occasion was an attempt at solemnity, Katherine and Michael rode their horses up and down the lines of knights. It frightened her how few knights were in her army, compared to the vastness of the army they were up against. She shook off the shiver of fear that crept up her spine. When the inspection was completed, Adam was called forward. He thanked them for their time and lauded the men for their good work.

"Your Majesties, would it be too much to ask for a reward for these men and their hard work?" The men looked at one another in shock. Why would Adam be so blunt with the Princess and her husband?

Katherine laughed. "If it pleases you."

Adam smiled. "A day off."

She looked puzzled. Michael shrugged.

"A day of play for those who have been working hard towards the coronation. We do not have many days left of winter. Therefore there are few days we can be fairly sure our enemy is not waiting at our doorsteps. Let us thank God for the days he has given us and celebrate with one another: life and faith and trust in our God."

KATHERINE'S KINGDOM: TO LOVE IN PEACE

The crowd was stunned at the quiet, yet solemn, speech. A moment passed before Katherine spoke again. "You may have your day. Two weeks from today. I appoint Adam as the leader in this venture. All questions may be directed to him." She turned her horse and stately, but quickly, fled. Michael nodded to all and turned his horse to follow hers.

He caught up with her in the stable. Edwin was putting her horse away in the stall as she rewarded it with a carrot for such good behavior. With the horse safely away, and Edwin's attention now on Michael's horse, the couple wandered away from the crowds.

"You seemed distracted today."

Katherine pulled her cloak closer to her. Today was cold, but not as cold as it had been. Her breath left little cloud wisps in the air as they walked through the snow. When she glanced back, there were footprints to match each crunching of snow as they passed. She didn't answer Michael's unspoken question.

"Adam spoke very eloquently."

"Yes. He did."

"He did a good job of presenting his point."

"Yes."

Michael began to grow frustrated. Their leisurely pace failed to match the conversation. Every tactic was blocked by a wall he couldn't scale.

"Katherine." He grabbed her hand to stop her from walking.

"Yes?"

"There's something wrong. You were rushing to get away at the end of the inspection. What was so wrong with Adam's proposal?"

"Nothing at all."

"Then why…"

"It's my birthday."

"Today is?"

She sighed. "No. Two weeks from today."

"Why does that upset you?" Michael examined her face for a clue to her despondency. But, she wouldn't look at him. Her face was downcast; and her hair fell in her face because of the slight breeze.

"I haven't celebrated it since Father left. He threw me a big party on my eighteenth birthday. It was my last birthday before the war…" She shook her head to remind herself to continue. "There was a great feast and celebrations throughout Adven. It was a time of celebration for all the people. The winter had been a calm one. The previous harvest had been good." Her eyes finally met Michael's. "My Father made an effort to make my birthday special. He always did, but this year especially. There were rumors of war on the outskirts of Adven, and he suspected the worst. As usual he was right. Two months later I waved goodbye and that was the last I saw him alive."

Michael touched her shoulder gently. He wished he could wipe away the pain in his young wife's eyes. What a life! She had everything anyone could want, but after her mother died…nothing had gone right.

"It will be alright, Katherine. I promise."

She shook her head. "Can you make the war stop? Can you bring spring? Can you raise my Father back from the dead?"

Gently, ever so gently, he pulled her close to him. Her warmth mixed with his own and he felt her muscles relax as she leaned into him. "I would if I could. How I wish I could!"

And then, Katherine cried. She let all her tears encompass her fears and her past. Her whole body racked with the sobs as she buried her face into her husband's shoulder. Some of the tears froze on her face, while others splashed onto his cloak. "I should have been there. I should have been there to save him. But, I couldn't save him. I couldn't save him."

Michael listened in silence. "It's not your fault your father died."

"Yes, it is."

"What could you have done?"

She pulled back. "I could have been there. Instead of sitting here waiting for letters that never came, I should have gone out and help fight. Then maybe I would have been able to save him…"

"But who would have run the kingdom while you were away? The Regents had almost given up on you after a few months. What would have happened if you had been gone for years? Katherine, there was nothing you could have done differently!"

"How do you know? You aren't God! You don't know!" she screamed and pushed Michael away from her. He tried to speak, but she covered her face with her hands and ran off through the snow. As the snowflakes started drifting down to the ground, he stood praying for his wife.

"What do I do now, God?"

Chapter Fifteen

Katherine handed over the details to Adam, just as she had promised. Everything went through him. Of course, this meant everything was scrutinized and analyzed once, twice, and as many times as he felt necessary. This was to be a celebration perfect in every way. It wasn't just meant to give the men a rest; it was meant to give them hope. As the dark days of winter enveloped the tiny kingdom of Adven, fear began to set in. No one knew how the war would end or where they would be a year from now. Would there even be a kingdom of Adven a year from now?

Adam understood the feeling that began to creep silently through the ranks. It was reflected in the seriousness of every drill. The lack of joy in the faces of the men and the quiet rustle of feet through crunching snow epitomized the fear. If they didn't do their drills or sharpen their swords, Adven would be lost. But, unlike those still serving the silent gods of their fathers, Adam and Edwin had hope. They poured their hope into the lives of those around them, filling the empty vessels with life and fulfillment. Each day was a new opportunity to share the hope they had found with those whose lives were devoid of hope.

Michael observed the same feeling creep through the servants of the house. They did their work well, but without feeling. Fear of darkness, fear of unsettling sounds, fear of the unknown world beyond the castle walls filled every action with distress. Was the enemy sneaking up on the castle as they washed the dishes? Was the crazy leader plotting their ruin as they swept the throne room? Was this the last meal they would eat as they peeled the potatoes for soup? The thoughts were almost overpowering for the poor hopeless people of Adven. Unknown things waited for them somewhere. War was one thing when it was in some battlefield far away. War was real when it was knocking on your doorstep.

The horror that filled the people filled their princess. As she sat in her room day after day looking out the frost-covered window, fear frosted her heart. Fear of the war. Fear of the man trying to kill her. Fear of death. Fear of this baby growing inside her. Fear of Michael's love ending. Would he ever forgive her? She had shut him out of her world on more than one occasion. With each new confession of past pain came the new pain of the secrets she bore. Tears were a constant in her eyes. Where would she be a year from now? Would she even be alive a year from now? Would this baby?

Katherine's mind was a whirlwind of fear that threatened to sweep her away. Her tears were tiny floods that sought to drown her in their unexpressed sorrow. Her heart broke when she saw Michael solemnly walking in the garden path, alone. She should be there to support him! She was his wife after all. But, the pain was too great to bear. She couldn't bear his pain in addition to her own. Honestly, she wasn't sure if she would ever be able to bear another's pain in addition to her own. Her love never died. In fact, it drove her to prove her love by doing everything perfectly. The room was always neat. His papers always in order. She was prompt for every meeting. Respectful in every council. She valued his advice and received his criticism with grace. But, her heart was so heavy. It was sealed up so tight that the love could not come out. Michael's eyes looked broken and empty when he looked at her. His heart was full of faith, and it was expressed in his unconditional love for her. Would she ever be able to accept it?

"Katherine?"

She pulled the blankets down so he could see her face. "I'm trying to sleep, Michael."

He paused. "I'm sorry to bring up past hurts. I'd make them all go away if I could."

"I know."

"Tomorrow is going to be hard on you." It was a fact, not a question.

She nodded silently.

"Thank you for going through with it." He leaned over to kiss her cheek.

She felt the baby kicking. The weight of her secret and her desperation for it to remain a secret troubled her, but she ignored her guilty conscience. "I'm tired, Michael." And with that final push accompanied by a small kick, she rolled over and closed her eyes.

"Katherine…"

"Michael, please. Just let me sleep."

She could feel him thinking about what to do next. Her heart ached for him to hold her. She wanted his comfort. But, there was a small secret that was turning out to be not such a small secret after all that sat between them.

"I love you, Katherine. You know that don't you?"

"Of course I do. I'm just tired."

"Sleep well, my love."

She closed her eyes shut to try and stop the tears trickling down her face.

The castle was decorated as festively as could be arranged. Colorful cloths hung on the walls, and the tables were covered with bright tablecloths. Everything was bright and happy. Blues, yellows, reds, and purples splattered the walls and clothing in the room. Everyone was happy and joy filled every heart. The women wore their best dresses and the men wore bright colors with their swords strapped to their belts, a constant reminder that this was still war.

Food covered the tables. Chicken, pork, and fish in all varieties of ways spanned the great table. Salads of every kind were present. Katherine had insisted they use whatever they needed. There were some who protested that this kind of celebration should wait for the coronation, but her quiet insistence rejected that thought. There was to be no shortage for anyone present.

Adam stood by the fire and watched the result of his handiwork. Everyone danced and laughed with each other. They ate of the food provided. Happiness was clear on every face. Michael even looked happy for a change. He moved among the people. A story here. A bite to eat there. A laugh. A dance. The king was comfortable with his people, and they with him. The only figure drifting through the day was Katherine.

She stood to one side. Speaking only when spoken to. Quietly observing her husband wander around through the people. Her face showed no emotion, whether joy or sadness. Only her eyes moved. They searched for something among the faces of the crowd, the never flickering eyes danced across the faces. Her eyes looked so empty; it made Adam shiver. He observed for as long as he felt he could possibly go on staring at those empty eyes before grabbing Michael, who was just walking past.

"Michael, is there something wrong with Katherine?"

The happiness flickered for a second. The pain was revealed in his eyes for one brief second and then was covered up by what was now revealed as false happiness.

"Why do you ask? Has she said something?"

Adam shook his head. "I was just watching. She seems a little distant."

Now anger flickered through the calm eyes. "What do you mean?"

"I didn't mean anything by it, Michael. I just wondered if there was something bothering her."

"Wouldn't I know that? I am her husband." The emotions were flooding the eyes now. Anger mixed with confusion mixed with pain danced around in the irises.

Adam once again observed silently. "You don't know do you?"

"You aren't always right, Adam. It's best to remember that." Before the king turned on his heel and marched off, Adam saw the truth in the flickering eyes and breathed a silent prayer for his young friends.

"Katherine."

She was startled from her reverie by the strange tone in Michael's voice. "What's wrong? Has something happened?" she asked, her voice filled with panic.

"That's what I would like to know."

"What are you talking about?"

He lowered his voice in an attempt to contain his emotion. "Adam was just interrogating me about you. Must you make it look like I don't know what's wrong?" He paused. "Actually, I might feel better if you would just tell me what's wrong."

"Michael, I…"

"No more excuses, Katherine. I love you too much to let you keep it from me any more. What has you so scared that you won't talk to me anymore?"

"Do we have to talk about this now? People are staring…"

"Let them." His voice returned to its normal concerned tone. "What's wrong?"

Here it was. An opportunity to be free from the secret. It truly was wrong for her to keep it, but she was so close. Six and a half months, only two and a half more to go. This baby was a part of her. She couldn't give it up…not when she was so close.

"Michael, there's nothing wrong. Please I can't tell you right now…" She covered her mouth, but it was too late. The secret was on the brink on being revealed. But not here! Not now! Not in front of all these people! What would they think?

He caught the contradiction. "Not right now?"

Katherine shook her head and squeezed her eyes shut. There was no place for tears on such a happy day. A happy day for everyone but her.

"But you will tell me?" He grabbed her shaking hands and held them in his own. They were rough and strong. Calluses covered the fingertips. These were hands that she loved. Hands that would someday hold their baby.

"I promise. Please just let me do it in my own time."

He nodded and turned to move away.

"Michael?"

The king turned back to look at his queen. She was standing there looking so beautiful. Her hair glowed from the firelight. Her dress sparkled with the gold weavings amongst the royal purple cloth. Her eyes sparkled with happiness. Even if she had not shared her secret, there was now proof that there was a secret. A small part of the burden had been lifted from her heart.

"I love you." And with that statement she flew into his arms and kissed him. There was no distance. There was no distraction. It was just the two of them. The way it had been when they were first married. "I've set you as a seal upon my heart, Michael. I promise I'll tell you everything."

"I'll love you until the day I die, Katherine." He held her close as the hall erupted in cheers. The people had been quieting observing their royalty's conversation and were pleased with the happy ending. The loud clapping covered up Michael's whisper. "Happy birthday, my love."

Tears rolled down Katherine's cheeks and she kissed her husband again, while the baby inside her leaped for joy.

Chapter Sixteen

"Are you getting excited? A real coronation. With a real king and a real queen!" Edwin said happily as he and Adam walked in the slushy snow. There had finally been a break in the weather, so some of the snow was starting to melt. The two men walked along, doing their rounds. They were a bit of an odd pair.

Adam was a well-trained knight. He had been one of the key protectors of Michael's little village. All the men looked up to him. He was respected and loved by everyone. Edwin was nothing more than an awkward and gangly teenager. He was happiest among his horses. He was a poor knight, and only continued his training because Adam believed he was good for more than taking care of horses. His red hair was a beacon of his mood. If it was combed, he was being serious and doing something he felt was important. If it was flying in every which way, the horses were very clean and happy.

"I've never been to a real coronation before," Edwin continued. "I'd never really left my farm until that man…" He shook his head and tried to erase those sad months where he was a soldier in an army not of his choice. Those months were the other reason it took all of Adam's encouragement for him to take up a sword and fight.

Adam put a hand on the boy's shoulder. "I am eager for Michael and Katherine to take up the throne. The kingdom of Adven will never be the same, of that much I am sure."

"They were born for this weren't they?"

Adam smiled. "Yes, Edwin. I believe they were."

They walked a few more paces before Edwin spoke again. "Adam, is everyone born for something?"

"Yes. I believe so."

There was another pause. "What was I born for?"

The pair stopped walking. Adam looked into his young companion's face. The pain and confusion was clear. Here was a boy who had left everything he had ever known. Everything he thought he knew was a lie. He'd met a God who cared for him. He'd met people who cared about him. But, he wasn't sure if he cared about himself yet.

"I don't know, Edwin. Someday you will though. God will make it clear for you."

Edwin sighed. "I wish He'd make it clear now."

The two continued to walk the rounds in silence as the snow silently melted beneath their feet.

"Two weeks really flew by, didn't it?"

Katherine jumped up from her chair where she'd quietly been letting out the seams of one of her dresses. The needle dropped to the floor and the dress dropped into the chair.

"I'm sorry! I didn't mean to scare you." Michael smiled as he retrieved the needle for her. His wife was a bit jumpy, and a bit slower moving of late. The stress of the past few months was clearing wearing down her defenses.

"It's alright. Just don't tell anyone their queen was afraid of a door opening and an unexpected voice." She smiled. "Or I'll have to prick you with my needle."

He held up his hands in mock defense. "Nothing to fear, milady." He bowed. "I am your sworn protector." He stood to his feet. "And your adoring servant." He leaned over and kissed her cheek.

"Thank you, good knight. And how may I be of service to you?" Her gentle laughter filled the room with sunshine, even more so than the sunshine streaming in through the window just behind her.

Michael smiled. This was his bride, the princess of her people, and the queen of his heart.

"Just wanted to tell you I love you. Is everything ready for tomorrow?"

"Yes. Why? Do you think I'm forgetting something?"

"No. I just want it to be perfect for you."

A shadow crossed her face. "It'd be perfect if my father was here."

There was silence in the room that was filled with Katherine's quiet pain. She still blamed herself for his death. Nothing Michael could say would ever change that.

"It wasn't your fault."

But he'd still try. "You say that. But you don't know."

He leaned down and looked into her pain-covered face. "Forget it for one day." He took her hands, careful to not be pricked by the needle. "This is the moment God has called you to. Live in it for all its worth. Enjoy everything God has to offer. He's given us this joyful time before the storm. Please," he looked into her cloudy eyes, "please don't let the day go by dwelling on what can't be."

"I'll try, Michael. Really." She flashed a smile. "It's your day too."

He grinned. "Just like a wedding, this coronation is all about the queen."

Katherine blushed. "Really, Michael."

The radiance of his smile was enough to light up the room.

Just then the wind blew open the window. The sunlight streamed into the bedroom, casting cheery shadows on the wall. Katherine walked to close it again and paused to look outside. The snow was melting on every walkway and parapet. Little green buds were beginning to poke out of the dark brown earth. It would be a beautiful spring, if not for the shadow of war.

"It's a beautiful day, isn't it?" Michael stood and put his arms around her waist. She felt the baby kicking and moving inside her in response to the additional warmth.

Just then Adam and Edwin walked by, continuing in their rounds. "They never stop working, do they?" Katherine said as she moved back to her chair.

Michael watched her and slowly nodded. "Just like someone else I know."

Stabbing her needle into her work, she laughed. "There's just too much to be done and so little time to do it!"

He played with the stray blond hairs tickling her cheek. "Don't you ever wish we didn't have to worry about coronations and wars and kingdoms? Don't you wish we could have met in the street somewhere and married and be worried about a family instead of the status of our knights and supplies?"

Violent kicking distracted her for a moment. The baby was restless. Or was he, or she, tired of being kept a secret for so long?

"Michael, I…"

A knock rapped on the door.

Michael sighed. "Enter." He rose and stood protectively behind Katherine's chair.

The soft footsteps accompanied the quiet creaking of the door. Eli's solemn face was revealed as he came the rest of the way into the room. "Your Majesties?"

"Yes." Michael gently laid his hand on Katherine's shoulder. She had come close to telling him the secret. He just knew it. If only Eli would go away…

"Your presence is needed in the Council Room. A final meeting with the Regents before the coronation."

He sighed and helped Katherine to her feet. "We'll be there in a moment."

The day of the coronation dawned bright and clear. No clouds made an appearance and the snow continued to melt. It was the first particularly warm day since fall. Not even a hint of chill in the air. The throne room was decorated for the solemn occasion. All of Adven's banners were hung on the walls. The bright purples and golds brought color to the gray stone walls. Each window let in the sunshine making the room appear bright and cheerful. A long purple carpet was laid out up the center of the room. The people who had come to see stood on both sides. Every commoner was joyful with bright hopes for their futures. The knights stood with a calm countenance covering their almost overwhelming happiness. The Regents stood in a line across the front. The Chief Regent stood in the middle of the two thrones. The one to his left was the Queen's throne with light purple and gold fabric draped on the back. The one to his right was the King's throne draped with gold and dark purple fabric.

Musicians started to play. Little village girls walked up the aisle dropping preserved flower petals on the carpet, giggling as they went. Adam and Edwin followed them. Adam carried Michael's crown, while Edwin carried Katherine's. They walked to their places beside their corresponding thrones next to the Chief Regent. When all was ready, their majesties entered.

Katherine came first, both because she was Queen and because she was the blood heir to the throne. Her golden hair was pale compared to her dress. It was a light lavender, with a golden cape that fell from her shoulders. She walked swiftly up the aisle her face fixed on the throne in front of her. When she reached the raised dais, she stepped lightly up to the throne platform. Silently, she stood before her throne.

All eyes turned to the doorway as Michael entered. He looked every inch the Prince that he was. His shirt was a dark purple, denoting his royal status. There was also a gold cape draped on his shoulders. Solemnly, he walked up the aisle. The people watched his every movement. He stepped up to the throne and stood facing the crowd before he grinned. A boyish expression crossed his face, like he'd just gotten his first pony. There were a few subdued laughs in the crowd, including Katherine's.

"Before you today, you see two people. Princess Katherine you have known all your lives. Many of you watched her grow up in these very walls. The daughter of our beloved King Andrew and Queen Aimi now stands before you ready to accept the throne." The Chief Regent took a breath before continuing. "The other you do not know as well, but he and his God have won our hearts. Michael is a Prince in his own right, the brother of King Evan, of Suffrom, whose wife we know is Katherine's sister, Queen Ralyn. It was a long and difficult process to get to this day, but we are here. With war at our doorsteps, there is no better couple to have standing before you."

The crowd interrupted the speech with their cheers. It took a few moments before they would be calmed. Michael flashed a smile at his wife, who responded with a giggle. Eli, who stood in the midst of the crowd, observed with a laugh of his own. "Just like children, they are. Grown up children."

Finally, the crowd grew quiet. "Thank you. I know you have awaited this day for many years. I promise not to prolong it." A shared laugh among the Regents, followed by a quick glare from their Chief. "But, this is a solemn occasion and certain standards have to be met." He turned to Katherine. "Princess Katherine, of Adven, do you promise to rule this land with righteousness?"

"I do."

"Do you promise to provide justice to your people in their time of indecision?"

"I do."

"Do you promise to live as an example to those before you?"

A brief scan of the room accompanied by a smile. "I do."

"Do you promise to uphold your husband as the King of Adven?"

A smile in his direction. "I do."

"Do you promise to care for your family forever as you would care for your kingdom?"

An unnoticeable pause. "I do."

"Do you understand that this is a lifelong commitment to rule and govern the kingdom of Adven?"

A final smile and a feeling of satisfaction. "I do."

Cheers from the crowd followed the Chief Regent's motion for her to sit in the throne. The cheers continued as he moved to his position next to Michael.

"Prince Michael, of Suffrom, do you promise to rule this land with righteousness?"

"I do." The boyish smile never left his face.

"Do you promise to provide justice to your people in their time of indecision?"

"I do."
"Do you promise to lead your men to war to defend this kingdom?" The smile changed to seriousness. "I do."
"Do you promise to live as an example to those before you?"
"I do."
"Do you promise to support your wife as Queen of Adven?"
A loving smile. "I certainly do."

A satisfied murmur spread through the crowd as the Regent raised his hands for silence.

"Do you promise to lead your family as you lead your kingdom?" His eyes locked with hers. "I do."

Michael sat as Adam and Edwin moved forward. The Chief Regent very carefully removed the golden tiara from the pillow. He moved behind Katherine's chair and set it on her head. The crowd erupted in cheers! The cheering grew louder as the Chief Regent removed the glimmering crown and placed it on Michael's head.

"Kingdom of Adven, your King and Queen!"

Michael took Katherine's hand and they descended the steps together.

"King Michael and Queen Katherine!"

They moved down the aisle once more, followed by Adam, Edwin, and the Regents. "Long live the King! Long live the Queen!" The cheer was repeated until they were out of sight of the crowd.

As soon as the sunlight hit their faces, Michael grabbed Katherine and pulled her into his arms. "We did it! Katherine, we did it!" He spun her in the air and watched as her dress and hair flew all about her. Her laughter was like rain drops sprinkling on his ears. She was so beautiful. The embodiment of every good thing. A drop of water distracted his joy, and he set her down.

"Are you crying?" He asked as he searched her face.

Katherine shook her head and wiped her eyes. "No, well, yes. I'm just so happy, Michael." She buried her face in his shoulder and let the happy tears cascade down her cheeks.

"Ready?" he asked after a moment.

She nodded. A quick wipe of her eyes and her smile was set firmly back in place. "I'm ready. Thank you, Michael."

A smile. "Thank you, my love." A quick peck on the cheek and Michael escorted his queen to the dining hall.

Chapter Seventeen

The table was set, once again, for a feast. Everyone who had attended the coronation was crowded into the hall. The food was even more lavish than two weeks before. The war looming on the horizon was the furthest thing from anyone's mind. The same joy that was present before, was present today. There were children laughing and prancing about, running in between their parents' legs. The knights were enjoying themselves and taking a break from their watchful vigilance. Even the servants who did not have the day off were enjoying themselves, conversing as they carried plates and trays to and fro.

Katherine and Michael sat at the head of the table, governing over the chaos. They smiled down on everyone who happened to pass by whether they were little children or retired knights.

"It's beautiful isn't it?" Katherine whispered.

"Yes. It's beautiful to see people so free and happy."

"Yes." She lowered her voice. "I hope they can stay that way."

Michael just looked at her. "Everything will be okay. God's knows what He's doing."

Their conversation was interrupted by a gentle tugging on Katherine's skirt. They looked down to see a small peasant child smiling up at them. It was a little girl with flaxen hair and bright blue eyes. Her dress had been mended many times, but was not in terrible shape. Her feet wore small brown sandals. In her eyes was the spark of childhood happiness. "Queen Katherine?"

"Yes," she replied. "What is your name?"

"Lillie."

"That's a beautiful name, Lillie."

"It's my mommy's name."

Katherine's smile widened. "Is there something you wanted to ask me?"

Lillie nodded.

"Go ahead."

"Now that you're a queen, Miss Katherine…" she bowed her head shyly.

"Go ahead, Lillie. Don't be afraid."

"Are you and King Michael going to have a little princess?"

Katherine blushed, but was luckily spared the horror of answering by Lillie's mother.

"Lillie! Leave the King and Queen alone! They are very busy today."

Michael waved away her fears. "She's no trouble. Lillie is a beautiful child, ma'am."

A quick nod and both mother and child were gone.

"What an odd question. Don't you think so, Katherine?" He turned to her. Her face was completely pale except for the blush spreading across her cheeks.

"Katherine?" Michael repeated, his voice edged with concern.

"Nothing. I'm just tired. Would you excuse me for a moment?"

He nodded, and she quickly and gracefully fled the room.

"I think everything went well today, don't you?" Michael said as he sat on the bed. The moon was shining into the dark bedroom, giving them just enough light to get ready by. Katherine was brushing out her hair and fluttering about the room, picking up stray objects dropped in their rush earlier that morning.

"Yes. Everyone seemed happy, and nothing went wrong. It was a perfect day." She reached down and picked up a lone shoe. Puzzled, she began to look for its pair.

"You seemed flustered after the little girl's question."

"Lillie?"

"Yes. Was everything alright? Did her question really upset you?"

Katherine felt the baby move. "No. I'm fine. It just caught me off guard." She continued to look for the missing shoe.

"I was worried about you," he said as he readjusted his position on the bed. Katherine's search had taken her under the edge of it, and he wanted to be out of the way.

"There's no need to worry about me. I'm fine," she insisted, still looking for the matching shoe. "Where could it be?"

"What are you looking for?"

She held out the one shoe she had. Michael smiled and pointed. "You're wearing the other one."

"Oh." Embarrassed, she looked down and saw the mate to the shoe in her hand, right there on her foot. "Forget that."

"Yes, Your Majesty." The shoe came flying at him, while he laughed.

"You're such a child. Why were you smiling so strangely during the ceremony?"

Knock. Knock. Knock.

The couple looked at each other. "Enter," they said simultaneously.

A wise old face peeked around the bedroom door. Eli smiled as he came all the way into the room. "Your Majesties." A short bow. "I hope I'm not disturbing you."

"Actually you saved my life," Michael smiled as the second shoe flew across the room. He looked at Katherine. "Now who's the child?"

"If I had another shoe I'd throw it," she said playfully.

Eli shook his weary head. "You are both children. Children at heart. Such a pity you must live in a grown up world."

The playfulness stopped. "Has something happened, Eli?" Michael rose from the bed, no longer looking like a child, but like the king he was.

"Not yet. One of the watchmen thought he spotted knights on the horizon. Adam has sent some to spy on whatever it was." A shrug. "It could possibly be some peasants having a belated celebration."

Michael shook his head. "Or an enemy spy trying to catch us off guard. Thank you, Eli, for your warning." He turned to his wife. "I should go be with the men." But, before he could step foot out the door, Eli stopped him with a gesture.

"There will be times for that. Tonight may be one of the few nights you two have together. Enjoy it. Be children for one more night." With tears in his eyes, he turned to Katherine. Stepping forward, his wrinkled hands took her firm young ones. "Promise not to grow up too soon, my child. I would miss you so very much."

"I won't, Eli. You are my only father now."

He shook his head. "No. Never forget your God. He is a far better father than I could ever be. Trust Him before you trust me." Eli stepped back to the door. "Sleep well, both my children. If anything happens you will be notified." With a final tear dripping down his cheek and a lonely glance at Katherine, he was gone.

Michael returned to his place on the bed and observed Katherine. She was deep in thought and had not moved since Eli left. "Katherine?"

"It had to come now. It couldn't have waited just one week until we could get established. Or even a month…or two months!" The last was said with enormous frustration and punctuated by her plopping into the chair.

"God knows what He's doing. Everything will be fine."

"Will it?" Tears were threatening to fall and clung to her lashes. "Will anything ever be fine again? Will there ever be peace? Will my people ever know God? Will we ever be able to have a family? A real one?" She gave up on trying to hold in the disappointment and burst into tears.

Michael rushed to comfort his wife. "I see little Lillie's question upset you more than you'd own. Look at me, Katherine." She looked into his eyes with questions filling her own. "I love you. Nothing will ever separate us. I will love you until the day you die. Katherine," he leaned close to her and whispered fiercely. "We will have a family. I promise you. We will have a family. And Katherine, our little girl will live in peace. She won't have to worry about her parents going off to war and never coming back. We will be here to raise her…together. I promise you."

"Michael, how soon do you want this to be true?" She could tell him. Now would be the time. He would be happy. His dream would come true! If only this silly war was over…

"When the war is over. We have to be sure there's a real peace for her. A peace that is free from fear. That is my promise to her." He kissed Katherine's cheek. "Let's go to bed. There's a big day ahead of us. Who knows what it will hold, My Queen."

Before she could say another word, Michael had helped her into bed and the candle was blown out. Darkness enveloped her and she wondered how she got herself into this mess.

"Michael?" The door creaked as it opened. Adam knew that the couple would be exhausted after their long day, but there was no other option. "Your Majesty?"

The room was dark. The predawn light was blocked from the room by the heavy drapes. Adam's candle lit up a small circle around him. As he moved the circle of light to the bed he smiled. Katherine and Michael were sleeping soundly in each others' arms. Their faces were peaceful and worry free. God willing, someday that peace would be as undisturbed in the daylight as it was in sleep.

"Michael?"

The king stirred in his sleep. He rolled over and lazily opened his eyes. "Adam?" He sat upright, suddenly alert. "Adam? What's wrong?"

"The scouts have returned."

"And?"

"We are surrounded."

Michael looked at him in disbelief. "How is that possible?"

Adam shook his head. "I don't know. There's nothing we can do about it now." He nodded toward the sleeping form still lying on the bed. "Should we wake her up?"

"Not yet." Sadly, Michael looked at his wife's sleeping body. "There will be time enough later."

"Time for what?" Katherine smiled sleepily at Michael as he stood up from the bed. When she saw Adam standing solemnly in the doorway, she became instantly awake. "Michael, what's going on?"

He sighed. "The war has returned."

Adam stepped forward. "They surrounded us. We are completely cut off."

"Was anyone hurt?" She started to get out of the bed than stopped. The terror screaming through her body was enough to make her head spin. The baby turned and twisted. "What are we going to do?"

Michael reached over and grabbed her hand. "Everything is going to be fine. We'll make it through this. I promise."

"I'll leave you two alone. I'm sure you'll want to formulate a plan." Adam stiffly bowed and left, closing the door behind him.

Katherine wanted to cry. Everything in her wanted to curl up in a ball and have Michael hold her. She wanted to get back under the blankets and sleep until the nightmare was over. "What are we going to do?"

"You knew this was coming."

"I know."

"You knew we would have to deal with this."

"I know."

"You knew this was part of our responsibility."

"I know!" She buried her head into her pillow and continued screaming, "I just didn't want to have to deal with it so soon! I didn't expect to be crowned queen one day and fight a war the next! I can't deal with it, Michael! I can't deal with it all!" She sobbed and sobbed and sobbed. There was no stopping the flood of tears running down her cheeks.

Michael said nothing for a moment. He watched her crying. "Honestly, it wasn't what I wanted either." He slipped back onto the bed beside her. "I wish we could just live happily ever after and never have rain or darkness. But that's not how it works. God has provided us this opportunity. We need to use it and take care of it. Adven is counting on us, Katherine. Please don't make me go alone."

The crying stopped. Slowly, she sat up and wiped the tears away from her eyes. She squared her shoulders and got out of the bed, walked to the closet and began to get dressed. "I won't make you go alone, Michael. Just promise me at the end of this neither of us will be alone. Will we make it?"

He wrapped his arms around her waist and pulled her close. "We will, my love. We will."

Chapter Eighteen

The Council Room door opened with a bang. Eli, Adam, and Edwin were already present. Nervously, they sat at the round table. It looked so empty with just the three of them. Like three against a storm of thousands, they sat awaiting their orders and willing to advise if necessary. King Michael and Queen Katherine entered solemnly. He held the chair for her and she sat. He took his place next to Adam. Eli reached over and patted Katherine's hand, assuring her everything would be alright. She was visibly shaken.

"Well, gentleman. What are we to do?"

There was silence in the room. Edwin tapped his foot anxiously.

"Well?" Michael gently coaxed.

"Do we have any options, but to fight?" Adam said with a sigh.

Katherine shook her head. "We could wait."

"What would that do?" Adam studied her while he waited for an answer. She was nervous, and the fear racing through her was clouding her judgment.

"We could prepare."

"We've been preparing."

"Well, he wouldn't expect it!"

"How can you be sure?"

Katherine breathed heavily. Her voice carried an edge as she replied, "What do you suggest, *Adam*?"

Michael placed his hand on hers and squeezed it. She made no response.

"I suggest we fight. What other option do we have?"

"That's the second time you've said that, Adam. Are you so sure we have no other option?" Michael's tone longed for compromise.

Adam slowly spoke, "No, I don't believe so. This man is out to destroy us. He will if we allow him. I suggest we show him what we are made of. We are ready for this moment! If we can crush him, then let us do it quickly. And if we cannot, then let us know so we may regroup and plan again!"

"We are talking about men's lives, Adam!" Katherine's voice trembled. "A direct assault would cost us more than we can spare! You're asking for us to send our men to be slaughtered!"

"There is always hope, Your Majesty." This was Edwin's first input into the discussion.

"Not when failure is certain. We are outnumbered five to one! How can we win against that?"

This made Adam angry. "Then you are sentencing us all to failure and conquest! We must try!"

"I won't risk it! There must be another way!" Katherine looked beseechingly to Michael, pleading with her eyes for him to agree.

The King sat thinking, planning, discerning. His eyes moved to each person at the table. They landed on Katherine. "It does appear there are only two options. To fight or to wait. If we wait, we are sentencing ourselves to a siege. We had prepared for this, but it is frightening for the people to sit and wait for seemingly certain death." He paused. "That leaves only the option to fight. It seems this is the course we must take for now. Adam," a glance at Katherine, "prepare the men. We must fight."

Katherine stood on the parapet looking down into the courtyard. The men were running back and forth in various directions, all preparing for war. She had been standing alone for an hour when Michael slipped behind her and placed his hands on her shoulders.

"I have to do what I feel is best, Katherine."

"I know."

"I love you, Katherine, and I always will."

Her eyes followed the chaos in the courtyard. "I know."

"Katherine," he squeezed her shoulder. "We need to go now."

A sigh. "I know."

Michael turned her body towards the stairs and started to walk away. When she didn't follow immediately, he turned back. "Katherine?"

She should tell him now. There would be no better chance. All the chances she had wasted before now! But, she could never get those times back now. All she had was…

"Your Majesties! The men are waiting for you." Adam's voice carried from halfway up the stairs. When Katherine came back from her reverie, the chaos in the yard has indeed stopped. Straight columns of horses and footmen covered the newly growing grass. Over on the other side of the castle she could just make out the new budding leaves on the garden trees. War and peace. Juxtaposed right before her eyes. She had no choice. The baby moved within her. There was no turning back now.

She turned and walked to Michael who was still waiting at the top of the stairs. Adam had already gone back down to the yard. The king and queen stepped hand in hand down the stairs to the horses that Edwin for them. With a light jump, they were both mounted and rode to the gathering group of men.

"Men, knights of Adven, we have before us today a crossroad." There was nervous shuffling of men's feet and horses' hooves. The men were eager to go and unprepared for a speech. Michael continued. "One path leads to destruction, and the other leads to life. Neither path is easy, but one offers hope to the hopeless and rest for the weary. The path of hope leads to God."

Now there were murmurs that raced through those gathered. The whispers threatened to drown out Michael's next words. "I know what you think! You think that no god can help us now! There is no help from that perspective!" He paused and took a deep breath. "You are wrong, however. There is a God who loves you and cares about you. He cares about Adven and he cares about Suffrom. His desire is to know you and for you to allow Him into your lives. Will you let Him? His path is not easy; there are rocky roads ahead. But, with Him comes hope and peace and freedom from fear."

"I want that!" a young knight cried out without thinking. The tension in the atmosphere settled on those in the courtyard as the young man pushed his way to the king. "I don't want to be afraid! I want to serve my country bravely; and if I must believe in God to do it, then I will!" He knelt at the foot of Michael's horse. "What must I do to know God and His peace?"

Before Michael could reply, another knight knelt quietly beside his friend. The look in his eyes filled Katherine's heart with joy. She was seeing new believers in God right before her eyes! In the midst of all this terror and trials, there was still hope for new life. More men came forward, and Michael prayed with them. Almost the entire army fell to their knees and accepted God as their Lord. When all had risen and tears had been dried, the men reformed their ranks and prepared to march.

The gates opened with a loud clang. Quickly, Michael and Katherine led the men onto the field. They separated into three ranks led by Michael, Katherine, and Adam. Edwin was standing somewhere on the castle walls with the archers.

The enemy lay before them stretched out like a sea of black knights. No standard led their charge, no king rode at the head. It was simply one frightening mass of swords and lances. With a loud cry, Michael charged forward. Katherine and Adam hung back. The first ranks were shattered by the sudden attack. A trumpet sounded in the enemy camp. The knights attempted to surround Michael's flank, but he retreated back to his own side before they had a chance. So far, so good. No man had yet been lost from Adven.

Katherine and Adam led the next charge, attacking the outskirts of the massive army. Again, the sudden change in direction caused confusion and chaos in the enemy ranks. They fell back, leaving their fellowmen slaughtered on the ground.

The blood made Katherine's stomach turn. *It's because of the baby.* She comforted herself with this thought. *I have not grown soft! And even if I have, I have no choice but to lead these men. I only hope I'm leading them to victory and not certain death.* The trumpet sounded for Adven and all three flanks charged.

This time the enemy was ready. They met the onslaught with fresh men. This time there were casualties on both sides. Loud battle cries rang in everyone's ears. The clash of metal on metal mixed with the sound of men and horses battling for their very lives filled the battlefield. Blood was everywhere.

Michael sounded the retreat. The remnant of the army pulled back, leaving disaster behind them. The enemy also retreated and attempted to regroup.

"Katherine! Adam!" Michael pulled the reigns of his horse to make it trot faster. Katherine and Adam pulled their horses up beside his and waited for him to speak.

His hand brushed the sweat from his brow. "They are stronger than I thought. We surprised them, but they'll be ready this time. How many have we lost?"

"I lost at least one hundred in that second charge. None in the first." Adam's face was indecipherable.

"About the same, I think I lost about seventy." Katherine focused on making her voice stop shaking. The baby was rolling inside her. If she didn't lose this child it would be a miracle.

"I lost fifty. We were the first charge that surprised them. They weren't given time to regroup. What is our next course of action?"

Adam shook his head. "It may not be up to us. They are preparing to attack it seems."

A trumpet ringing proved his words. The three leaders moved quickly back to their men. The wounded were left at the castle, and those still capable of fighting returned to the charge. Before they were properly prepared, the clash came. The black knights attacked with a vengeance. They were out for retribution. Angry voices yelled at the faces of the young knights of Adven. Trying not to show their fear, they returned every blow for every blow.

The battle was turning for the worse when Michael called the retreat. "To the castle!" Horses and men flocked to the gates, and the gatemen worked as fast as they could to close the huge oaken doors. Katherine looked behind her to make sure all the men made it inside. The mass of black knights following behind them was overwhelming. Fear gripped its icy hands around her heart. Her breath came in short little gasps as she gripped the reigns of her horse to her chest. The baby kicked violently. Every movement of her horse made her body jolt with shock and pain. How would they ever make it out alive?

The slamming of the doors interrupted her thoughts. She heard the whistle of the archers as they shot at those closest to the door. There were short cries of pain and the sound of stampeding horses turning back around to return to camp. They reminded her of a proud cat returning to his dish of milk after he has chased the mouse back to its tiny hole. She felt about as big as a mouse and just as frightened.

"Katherine! Adam!"

She jerked upright in the saddle and turned her horse to face her husband's voice as he rallied the troops. His face was as hard as a stone. There was a small cut on his cheek that was starting to bleed. Quickly, her fear turned to concern for Michael.

"Michael, you're bleeding," she whispered as she pulled a handkerchief from her sleeve.

"Don't worry about it. How bad was it?"

"We lost a lot. I think everyone made it inside though. Michael, there were so many of them…"

He looked at her with discernment in his eyes. "It will be okay. I promise."

With a flick of his reigns, he was off again. She sat watching him ride away to inspect the damage. Adam was already moving among the men, helping bandage wounds and bring comfort to those who had lost friends. Dismounting, she allowed Edwin, who had appeared out of nowhere, to take her horse to the stable. Everything seemed to be in a daze. Was this how her father had felt every day he was fighting the war? Now it was her turn to feel the heartache. Katherine felt sick. The baby was kicking. Did he or she know what was going on outside?

Eli stood quietly observing off to one side. He watched Katherine as she moved from one emotion to another. And then he saw it, a quick movement of her hand to her stomach, protective yet revealing the secret he had suspected for so long. In the next moment he was by her side looking at her startled face.

"May I speak with you a moment, Your Majesty?"

A quick nod and they were headed to the garden. Her hands trailed on the little buds that poked out from the trees. With eyes filled with a longing for peace, she turned to face him. "What did you want to speak to me about, Eli?"

"Why didn't you tell him?"

Her face flushed with embarrassment. "I don't know what you're talking about."

His eyes hardened with the familiar fatherly expression. "Yes you do."

Bright red embarrassment covered her entire face. She fidgeted and then turned away. "I should be getting back. They might need my help with the…"

Eli grabbed her wrist and stopped her from moving. "Katherine."

His tone arrested her with it's compassionate and concern. "I have everything under control." Her heart was breaking. If she didn't get away quickly it would all be over. "Please let me go."

"I think you should tell him. Haven't you kept it from him long enough?"

The baby kicked inside her. Why was it so restless today? Well, there was a war going on, both in Adven and within Katherine's heart. "I can't, Eli. He doesn't want it right now. There's a war going on! How could I do that to him?"

That firm hand never left her arm. "He's going to find out eventually."

Anger laced her reply. "I know! There's nothing I can do about it! Just let me fight this war and then everything will be fine!"

Eli shook his head. He released her hand. "There's a far greater war going on inside you right now, Katherine. Trust God. You've done so well so far. Don't give up so close to the end."

"This war's been going on for two years. I'm not sure it will ever end." With a twirl of her skirts she was gone, angrily marching to the kitchen to help get dressings for the wounded. Eli was left standing in the garden with tears rolling down his face. "God, please help her. She can't find You now, but help her to see. She needs You, God. Please… help her."

Chapter Nineteen

Again there was a meeting of the minds in the Council Room. Katherine and Michael sat side by side at the head. Around the rest of the room were Adam, Edwin, and Eli. They had been talking for hours, going over every possible strategy. Nothing seemed plausible. Every plan had more then one problem with it, lack of men being the main concern.

"We are simply outnumbered! There is nothing that will solve that problem," Katherine sighed and leaned back in her chair. The baby was still kicking inside her and it was becoming too much for her to bear. "What can we do that will not cost us the lives of every single one of our men?"

Adam shook his head. "You have a point, but we cannot give up. That is not an option. To give up would mean to surrender." A quick glance at the king and queen. "It would mean surrender to him. Adven would be doomed to a life of servitude to whatever his wants and wishes might be."

Edwin remained silent. Secretly, he was frustrated. If he still had a part to play in this story; he certainly didn't know what it was. Running a hand through his ragged red hair, he sighed.

The conversation continued in circles for a few more minutes before all five fell silent. No one had any new ideas to offer. There was no magical explanation that appeared. God did not remove the enemy from outside their door. They still were facing inevitable destruction.

Slowly, Michael stood. He addressed the room with resignation in his voice. "I believe we have no choice but to fight tomorrow as we did today. I will spend the night in prayer and would suggest that the rest of you do the same."

There were nods around the room. Katherine placed her hand on her stomach, trying to calm the restless spirit within her. This would be a long night.

The door creak as it opened. It had been awhile since she'd been in here. Her dress swept the dust on the floor in little circles as she walked to the window. With a quick motion, the window was open and the sunlight shone on Katherine's pale face. Tears were running freely down her cheeks. She was scared.

Another quick motion and she was moving along the wall, feeling for the spot. A click and the secret room opened up. The long bench all around the room was still there. Ralyn's cushion was sitting where it always was. The other pillows and cushions were stacked at various places for easy access no matter where she chose to walk, or sit, or stand.

She knelt to the ground and wiped a few of the tears from her face. The fear racing through her heart never left. She didn't know where Michael was. He had left almost immediately after their council to pray, just like he said he would. Now, it was her turn to take her fears and give them to God.

"God?" Her voice sounded empty in the quiet room. She brushed some loose strands of hair from her face. "I know I haven't talked to You in awhile. I've been busy. I mean, that's no excuse but…" She was rambling. *Get to the point, Katherine!* "I need You now, God. With that crazy man on our doorstep and more knights going to their deaths tomorrow and this baby trying to jump out of me…" The baby kicked to punctuate her remark.

"I guess what I'm trying to say is that I can't do this alone, God. I tried that. I tried to take care of Adven while my father was away, but I just made everyone miserable. I wanted to save him when I thought he was dead, but I was too late." More tears. "I didn't plan to fall in love with Michael. I guess that's the only good thing in this whole mess I'm in. But, now he's caught up in a war that doesn't even concern him, nor Adam, nor any of the other men who came with us! What did they do to deserve to suffer, God? They've been captured, gotten lost, gone for weeks without food, and for what? A girl who married their leader whom they barely know. What did I do to deserve that kind of loyalty, God? I don't deserve anything!" Here she completely broke down.

She didn't know how long she knelt on the floor crying. Sob after sob after sob racked her quaking body. The tears flowed down her face like a waterfall and would not stop. Even if she had wanted to, nothing could stop her sorrow as it escaped from her body in one long cry.

When she could breathe normally again, she sniffled, wiped her eyes, and tried to continue. "I'm sorry about that, God. I didn't mean to interrupt our conversation. But, I guess I needed that. It felt good to just tell You about all the things I've been thinking since this all started. Has it only been a year? It feels like it's been ten! What would I be now if all that hadn't happened? Where would I be?

Well, I wouldn't have married Michael. I know that much! I wouldn't be pregnant! That's for sure. But, I also wouldn't have met Adam or Edwin. Eli wouldn't be a believer, nor would the Regents or any of the other knights. It took Michael to lead them to You."

She shifted uneasily, trying to keep her feet from falling asleep. "What else should I say, God? Do You want to hear about how scared I am? I'm scared for the battle tomorrow. What if we don't win? What will become of Adven? Everything I've been working for years to protect will be gone. What then? What will become of Michael and the baby and I?"

Another pause. She was coming to the hard part. "I guess that's what I'm afraid of most, God. The baby. It's funny how such a little thing can change so many things. This baby has changed how I think about myself. I thought I was ready to be Queen. But, how can I be a queen if I can't even take care of the baby inside me? I'm not ready to be a mother! Although, if you think about it, being a queen is like being a mother to thousands of people. Therefore, if I can do that, I can take care of one little girl…or boy."

A breath. "But, Michael doesn't know yet! Why didn't I tell him? Why didn't I tell him! I should have told him as soon as I was sure. But, that would have changed everything! He would have tried to shelter me like Evan did to Ralyn. I couldn't deal with that. How did I even manage to keep it hidden for eight months? Well, I technically have one month where I can still tell him. I have time, don't I?" The baby kicked. Her hand went to her stomach. "I can feel it. Isn't that just a miracle in itself, God?"

She paused for a moment just reflecting on the wonder of the baby growing inside her. Katherine knew she loved it. She knew that everything would be okay. She felt peaceful about everything. "Is that You, God? Are You the one giving me peace? I guess that's what I needed, isn't it? Peace. It's amazing how one thing can change everything, just like this baby. Will everything work out, God? Will everything be okay? Michael says it will be. I just wondered what you had to say on the matter."

Silence met her request. She heard nothing, but she still felt at peace. "Okay, God. I guess I'll just have to keep trusting You. I know that it will all work out just the way You want it, what ever that means. Take care of Michael, Adam, Edwin, Eli, and all the men. Take care of this baby too, God. It needs all the help it can get!"

Quietly, she got up, closed the secret door, and closed the window. With one last look around the room filled with her childhood memories, she got ready to close the door. Her eyes flickered to the portrait of her mother up on the wall. Katherine smiled. "I know you'd be proud, Mother. I'll make you proud."

Night came sooner than anyone wanted. The fires of the enemy camp lit up the grassy opening just outside their gates. Their laughter and loud voices trickled through the walls causing everyone to cringe with the anticipation of tomorrow's battle. Katherine lay in her bed praying Michael would come in soon. It seemed important that she spend tonight just wrapped in his arms. She didn't know what tomorrow would bring, but she knew that God was in control. Her prayers had done that much good. She felt absolutely at peace about the whole situation. If they lost, everything would be okay; that was all she knew.

The candle on the night table almost blew out when the door opened. Michael peered around the door to see if she was still awake. "I've been waiting for you."

His face was worn, but it lit up when he heard her voice. Coming to the bed, he crawled under the covers, took her face in his hands, and kissed her. "I love you."

"I love you too." Katherine buried her body into his open arms. They stayed like that for a moment, just resting in each other's love. Then Michael spoke.

"I can't promise what will happen tomorrow."

"I know."

"I can't seem to hear from God."

"I have."

There was a pause. "What did He say?"

"He didn't say anything. He just gave me peace." She rolled over so her eyes looked into Michael's. "I'm at peace about tomorrow. For the first time in months I feel like everything will really work out for the best."

A smile covered Michael's face. "I'm happy for you. I'll trust that God will give me that peace too."

They leaned into one another again. A few more solitary moments passed.

"I love you," Katherine whispered.

"I love you too," Michael whispered back. A few minutes later, he could feel her quiet breathing and the soft sound of her sleeping. "I love you, Katherine."

He moved and repositioned himself so he could sleep and still keep her in his arms. A bump on his hand startled him. Michael looked down at Katherine. She was still sleeping and didn't seemed to have kicked him. Puzzled, but too tired to try and figure it out; he wrapped his hands around her waist and fell asleep again.

Chapter Twenty

The day dawned bright and clear. The sun was shining on the newly growing grass. If it hadn't been a perfect day for war; it would have been the perfect day for a picnic. Katherine dressed quickly and buckled her sword tightly around her waist. There had been no incidents with it yesterday, nothing like the blinding light the night they were escaping; so, she was not worried about anything so frightening happening again today. In fact, she was not worried about anything. The peace that had overwhelmed her yesterday was with her still. Michael had risen early, to pray he said. She hadn't seen him since before dawn. She prayed that the peace she had would fill him as well. He had seemed distracted that morning, as though plagued by an elusive thought.

There was hustle and bustle all around the castle as the knights prepared for battle once more. They knew that today would be the day of either victory or defeat. Either way, they would do their best for their King and their country, as well as their newfound God. Her shoes made soft sounds on the grass as she walked about the courtyard, calling out a hello or flashing a smile. The knights responded to her happiness with their own. Even Eli smiled as he watched Katherine roam confidently around the preparations. "She has found God once again," he said to himself. "That is good. She will need all the help she can get today. It will not be an easy one."

Edwin was wandering around as well, tending to the horses. He'd spoken to Adam that morning and was determined to ride to battle today. Unfortunately, Adam didn't agree. "You're still too inexperienced. Stay with the archers. They need someone to lead them."

"The archers are more than prepared to take care of themselves!" Edwin insisted. "I felt so helpless yesterday. You said I still have a part to play. How can I play it if I am stuck behind the castle walls?"

Adam hated to agree with the boy, but he was right. However, the stubborn concern he had would not go away. In the end, Adam won. Edwin would stay with the archers. Muttering to himself, Edwin had gone off to help the knights with their preparations. Secretly, he still wondered if there was a part for him to play, even if it was a small one.

Overall, everyone was doing his or her best to prepare for the inevitable. There would be a battle today, whether they wanted it or not. Out of this battle would come a victor and a loser. If Adven won, the kingdom would be saved and peace would be restored. If the false king won, their lives would be changed forever.

A trumpet rang loudly and called for the assembly of the knights. Katherine mounted her horse and set it trotting toward the gate. Michael gave no speech today. He sat patiently waiting for her with the sun glinting off the golden circlet denoting him as king. Katherine had one just like it on her head, denoting her as queen. They both looked like the royal couple they were. Her horse almost pranced up to Michael's horse. The day could not have been any better, were it not for the fact that the gate was about to open onto a bloody battlefield. Still peace reigned in Katherine's heart. She flashed a smile at Michael to encourage him. He drew his horse right up next to hers and leaned over to whisper.

"I love you, and I will always love you. Love as strong as death, right, Katherine?"

"Right. I'll love you just the same no matter what happens. I love you, Michael."

"I love you too." With that he leaned over and kissed her on the cheek. The men behind them clapped and cheered. Katherine blushed. Just then, Adam rode up beside them.

"The gatemen and the trumpeter are ready when you are, Your Majesties." He bowed and moved his horse back with the men. The knights would march as one today, with their King and Queen in the front.

A nod from Michael and the gate opened. The trumpet sounded and the army marched forward. The people hanging out of the windows of the castle cheered, as did the archers led by Edwin. It was a joyful sound, ironic for such a bleak day. They were outnumbered and weak, but there was joy in their hearts as they marched to an unknown fate.

The enemy stretched out once again on the grassy open space before them. The sun was to Adven's advantage, as it was in their opponent's eyes. Katherine sat straight up in her saddle. She hardly moved a muscle. Instinctively, she drew her sword as the two lines approached each other. Suddenly, a bright flash reflecting partly from the sunlight, but mostly from her sword, filled the battlefield. The enemy line paused as they were momentarily blinded. Glancing quickly from Michael to the blinded knights across from them she screamed, "Now!" And raising her sword she took advantage of the momentary distraction. She charged forward, slashing madly with her sword. The gallop of Michael's horse was right behind her, along with the rest of the Adven army. The clash of battle was all around her as she was swept further away from the safety of the castle. All around her people were falling as she fought. Her sword was swirling like a baton around her. The space between her and her attackers was growing when suddenly she realized something terrible. In her first charge, the whole army had followed her. But, after the initial distraction and the subsequent battle; the army fell back, completely unaware that she was still in the midst of her battle fury. Now, she was completely surrounded!

Edwin saw it all from the parapets where the archers stood. He watched the charge go seemingly well at first, but then fall back. He saw the sun glinting off Katherine's sword and the golden circlet. That circlet ensured that she would be killed momentarily if someone did not help her. Suddenly, Michael looked as though he would charge single handedly back into the battle, but Adam pulled his horse in front to stop the king from attacking rashly. The argument couldn't be heard, but it was clear that Michael would not allow Katherine to die without a fight; and Adam would not allow the king to charge to his death.

In one moment, his mind was decided. Without a second thought, Edwin rushed down the stairs to the stable to grab his own horse. It was not the biggest or the best, and therefore had not been chosen to go into battle. Edwin had already saddled her because it felt like the right thing to do. Now he was immensely glad of that decision as he mounted quickly and went charging through the gates. His bow was still on his back, completely useless in the open battlefield, he thought. However, he had managed to unsheathe his sword and came bearing down on the army of Adven with sword in the ready. Startled knights backed out of his way; Edwin was an excellent horseman. In fact, he charged right in between Michael and Adam, giving neither the opportunity to stop him. With Adam's voice ringing in his ears he charged into the middle of the clash, desperate to save Katherine.

Queen Katherine was swinging her sword with all her might, taking out everyone within reach. Her thoughts weren't on Michael, the baby, or Adven. She was concentrating on staying alive! Her heart beat wildly and she thought about passing out, but then she'd be dead. Her sword arm was growing tired. Everything was starting to spin. Another few moments and she would have to focus on keeping her eyes open. Suddenly, there was more yelling behind her. She whirled around ready to face a new opponent and found Edwin, swinging a sword in every direction, coming to her rescue. In no time, he'd cut through the enemy line and forced her to retreat. Not that she needed much convincing.

KATHERINE'S KINGDOM: TO LOVE IN PEACE

The trumpet sounded the retreat for the opposing army. Exhausted, Katherine and Edwin returned to the waiting company. Michael rode forward immediately.

"Are you okay?"

"Yes, I'm fine. When I get my breath back, I'll be sure to thank Edwin for saving my life."

"I'll be sure to thank him as well."

"No thanks is necessary." Edwin rode up to the whispering couple, having overheard the conversation. "I was just playing my part." With a cluck to his horse, he turned and rode over to Adam who was smiling, revealing the deep affection he had for the boy as well as the intense pride that threatened to burst from his chest at any moment.

There was not another moment to think before the trumpet was sounding and they were charging once again. The clash of battle rang over the whole countryside. Knights fell to the ground on both sides. When the retreat was finally called, the men of Adven were tired and becoming discouraged.

"What's the plan?" Katherine called over the ruckus of retreat. Michael could barely hear her over the noise. She was looking at him waiting for an answer he didn't have. They couldn't keep charging and retreating. What good would that do? However, he knew there was no better plan today than there was last night.

"I don't know," he whispered. "God, give me a plan. I don't know what to do. I can't keep sacrificing these men, but I can't surrender. My hands are tied. Just tell me what to do!" As there was no immediate answer to his prayer, he turned to Katherine's upturned face. Her eyes were shining with the light of battle and the hope of victory. Where was this peace coming from? She'd never looked so beautiful to him as she did in that moment.

"It's okay if you don't have a plan. Love as strong as death, remember? I won't leave you, no matter what happens." If there had been a moment, she would have kissed him. As there wasn't, she simply smiled. The baby kicked inside.

Michael returned her smile and looked at the knights bringing the wounded from the battlefield to the castle. There were so many wounded! And there had been so few to start with! How could they ever face such odds?

"Princess Katherine!"

A stranger's voice echoed over the bloody grass. A single knight from the enemy's camp was coming forward with a scroll of parchment in his hand. His face was stern and hard. He spoke in a deathlike monotone that sent chills down Edwin's spine.

"It's the chief's right hand man, his brother," Edwin whispered to Adam. "He's the one who leads the warfront. His brother may be their 'king', but he's no fighter. He's a coward." Fearing that the approaching stranger heard him, Edwin ducked behind some of the men.

"Princess Katherine! To avoid unnecessary bloodshed, the King has offered these conditions of surrender: complete and total surrender of the lands and ruling of Adven, offer of servitude from both yourself and your husband, all future children immediate slaves to His Majesty, and revocation of all claims to the throne both now and in the future."

Edwin, still hiding behind those in front of him, heard these terms of surrender and nearly growled. The audacity! That coward! How dare he come and offer such unacceptable terms! And to even think that they would surrender!

Michael was about to speak, but the man interrupted. "My business is not with you. It is with the Princess Katherine."

"You mean Queen Katherine." And Katherine herself appeared. Her dress was torn and bloodstained from the battle. Her horse was breathing heavily. But, with the sun shining off her crown and her raised sword, she looked exactly like a queen. "I am no longer the little girl your chief knew. My father is dead and gone. You, whoever you are, have no business with me save surrendering yourself. It was you who attacked Adven for no reason but revenge! It was you who murdered hundreds of thousands of innocents! It was you who killed my father!" With each statement she rode closer and closer until her sword was almost on the knight's neck. Then she pulled back. "But, I believe in a God of mercy." She sheathed her sword and offered her hand. "Here are my terms of surrender: you and your men leave and never return. Your weapons remain here on the battlefield and you leave immediately. The offer is only open now. Take it or prepare to fight to your deaths."

The man looked at her outstretched hand for a moment and then drew his sword. In another minute, Katherine would have been dead; but an arrow flew through the air and killed the man where he stood. The whole army whirled around to see Edwin standing with his "useless" bow drawn and looking as if he were about to faint. His face paled and Adam caught him before he collapsed. With a smile on his face, the older man said, "Good job, my son. You have indeed played your part."

But, the war was not over yet. Seeing their leader shot down and knowing that whoever killed the Queen first would be the new leader, the army charged forward. They all raced toward Katherine and Michael who were fighting side by side. The knights of Adven responded instantly to the threat and many did not even reach the King and Queen before they met their deaths.

How long this went on no one knew. Michael and Katherine remained fighting side by side and back to back until they felt they would collapse. Still, there were always new knights coming from behind the lines. Everyone was tired and there was no sign of the end coming quickly. With no leader to sound their retreat, the army just continued to come in wave after wave of fresh knights coming to try their hand.

"Michael! I'm not sure how much longer I can hold out!"

She turned to hear his response and found that the two of them had become separated at some point. The army of Adven had consequently split in half in an attempt to protect both leaders. There was no time for strategy, just survival. Katherine swung her sword and knocked down one man, only to have him replaced by two more. It was the same everywhere she looked. It seemed defeat was unavoidable.

Suddenly, a trumpet ringing across the glade. It was not Adven's; nor was it the enemy's. "Where is that coming from?" Katherine screamed in frustration. She was completely surrounded once again. Her sword worked like a whirlwind swinging at anything that came close. That didn't seem to deter the knights attacking her. The trumpet continued ringing in the distance, quickly coming closer and closer until…

The trumpeter broke over the top of the hill off to their right. The standard bearer came right up behind him and the wind caught the flag unfurling it to reveal: the flag of Suffrom! King Evan had come to their rescue! A moment later the entire army of Suffrom was spilling onto the battlefield. King Evan himself was leading the charge into the confused enemy before them. If the knights had been in disorder before, now they fell into complete chaos. Some started fleeing into the woods. Others still continued to doggedly attack Katherine and Michael. Others turned their attention to King Evan, figuring to take him while he was first entering the fray. Adven's knights used the distraction to dispatch with the confused enemy who had no idea which direction to turn.

Katherine felt the knights around her letting up a little and she started to breathe a little easier. As she looked around, she saw Edwin fighting to her right. He had obviously recovered from his brief fainting spell and was now doing significant damage to anyone who tried to get near her. On her left, Adam was doing the same for anyone daring to approach Michael. His sword swung in brilliant curly cues and took down many a valiant knight. The battle was indeed turning in their favor. She couldn't see King Evan, but she could she his knights mixed among her own. They were pushing the enemy back from the castle walls. It seemed victory was near at hand!

Then the unthinkable happened. Just when it seemed that the war would soon be over and everyone would make it out alright, Katherine turned to see Michael struggling to free himself from the grip of one determined knight who'd caught hold of his sword arm. Seeing the King almost defeated, many knights turned their attention to unhorsing him. Before she had a chance to scream, Michael had been pulled from his horse, his sword taken from him, and immediately pulled underneath a sea of fighting people.

"MICHAEL!!!!!!!" Her voice rang above all the chaos around her. Both Adam and Edwin heard her distress and turned their attentions to rescuing their king. Many of the knights of Adven and Suffrom did the same. Katherine herself turned to charge through those immediately surrounding her. She raised her sword and a brilliant flash erupted, sending those attempting to attack her sprawling on the ground. Not stopping to ponder, she swept through the next layer of knights and rushed to her husband. She couldn't see him through the teeming mass of people. When she finally pushed her way through, she wanted to burst into tears.

It was just like in her nightmare all those months ago. He lay sprawled on the ground with unseeing eyes open to the world. There was blood everywhere and she couldn't tell which wound was the most significant. There were too many to count. His clothes and the ground around him were stained red.

The whole world seemed to stop and it was just Michael and Katherine. Every happy moment they'd spent together flashed through her mind. Then some of the sad times pushed their way in. She wanted to burst into tears and collapse on the ground, but that wasn't an option. She could feel the baby, their baby, kicking inside her. Nothing would ever be the same again.

A hand touched her arm. It was Adam. He'd finally reached her and seen Michael lying on the ground. He pulled her away from the distressing scene.

While her world had stopped, the battle had been won. The knights of Suffrom had saved them. No one had found King Evan yet. They didn't know whether he was alive or dead. Now that he knew where Michael was, Adam summoned knights to bear the King to the castle.

"Katherine?"

She didn't respond. At some point she had dismounted and her horse had been led away. She didn't remember that happening, but how could she now be standing on the blood red grass where her husband lay dying just a moment before? She didn't even hear Adam's question.

"Katherine? You've got to snap out of it! Your people need you!"

Still no response.

"Katherine!"

She finally looked at Adam with tearful eyes. "He's dead, Adam. I watched him die and I couldn't do anything about it."

"Katherine!" He grabbed her hands and held them in his own. Her sword had long ago fallen unheeded to the ground. "Michael is not dead!"

It didn't register. "I watched him die. I couldn't even say goodbye."

"Katherine!" Adam had to shout in her face to get her to look at him. "Michael is not dead! Not yet anyway. There is hope for him!"

"Hope?"

"Yes! Eli is with him now doing everything in his power to keep him alive."

"He's alive?" It finally dawned on her. "He's not dead? He's alive! Michael's alive!" She threw her arms around Adam's neck and kissed him on the cheek. Now the tears were falling down unhindered. She picked up her sword, wiped it on the grass, and sheathed it. She would have started off to the castle immediately if a knight had not appeared just then with a solemn look on his face.

"Your Majesty?"

"Yes?" Her face fell when she saw the knight's serious expression.

"We found King Evan. He was overtaken in the first attack." The knight lowered his eyes to the ground.

"Is he…"

"Dead? Yes. Many swords and spears pierced him. There was no chance for him, but we believe he probably died without much pain."

The tears that had been joyous now turned to sorrow once again. What would she tell Ralyn? What about their baby who was just a few months old? "Bring him to the castle. We will prepare the body and send him home. He would want to be buried in Suffrom."

As soon as the knight turned away to follow her instructions, she felt Adam's hand on her arm again. "Come now, my Queen. You have done all you can do here." She allowed herself to be led away from the battlefield. When they arrived at the castle, Eli made sure she went to her room and immediately went to bed. Katherine fell asleep instantly and slept until the next day.

Chapter Twenty-One

Queen Katherine stood on the parapet watching the men take care of the battlefield. There were, unfortunately, many graves to be dug and it was not a pleasant work. Better to get it done and over with quickly. But, she wasn't really watching the men work or the knights cleaning their weapons or the children running freely in the courtyard. Her mind was on the pale figure she had seen yesterday lying on the battlefield. Eli had not allowed her into the room where Michael lay. "He needs rest. He's far from healed yet. If you feel you want to help him, go and pray." So that was what she was doing. Standing alone on the parapet with the wind blowing her breezy blond hair out of her face and rustling her skirts; it seemed the perfect place to pray.

"God, You gave me such peace. I thought You said everything would be okay. Well, I guess You didn't say that. I said that. But, I thought that since You gave me peace You would make everything else work out as well."

She moved from leaning on the wall to pacing back and forth.

"Yes, we won the battle. The men are still searching for the chief, but if Edwin is correct, the second in command is dead. That's some good news at least. But, King Evan is dead. Michael is dying! This baby is kicking frantically like it wants to escape. All this mess can't be good for him...or her. That just complicates everything, God."

Sighing, she stopped pacing and looked out at the trees that made up the beginnings of the forest. The little creek she and Ralyn used to play in as girls was hidden somewhere out there. So wasn't the little forest path they used to take walks on. It all reminded her of a simpler time, before the war started.

Pausing she looked at the road that led away from the castle. It snaked around the forest and towards the little village that was about ten miles down the way. Eventually it would break off into different sections leading to all the various parts of Adven and Suffrom. Just now there was no one on it. Or was there? Dust seemed to be flying all around just beyond the bend. The top of a carriage appeared. Then the horses leading it. Then the knights guarding it. It wasn't a big party, but it was obviously someone important because the carriage windows were covered and there was a contingent of knights that followed on all sides. The wind again caught the banner flying from one of the standards and the flag of Suffrom was unfurled. Instantly, Katherine knew who it was and rushed down the stairs and out the gate to meet her.

Ralyn, Queen of Suffrom and sister of Katherine descended the steps of the carriage cautiously. She had a little baby in her arms, no more than three or four months old. Her smile of greeting turned to a look of astonishment when she saw what was going on around her. Katherine continued running to her, undaunted. She threw her arms around her sister and let the tears fall into her hair and onto her dress.

After a moment, Ralyn pulled back. She always had been more withdrawn and introspective. "What happened?" Her horror grew in intensity as she looked around and took in first the bloody battlefield, than the men moving solemnly about their work, and finally Katherine's tearstained face.

"The war. It came right to our doorstep."

"And?"

"It's over now. The knights are looking for the instigator to avoid further trouble. He couldn't have gotten far." Katherine was surprised by how detached she felt. This man had personally tried to kill her! How could she feel so empty?

"Where's your husband?" Ralyn looked around for someone who looked like a king. The men closest to her had overheard what she said and paused, waiting for Katherine's reply. Everyone was worried for their young king.

"Eli is with him. He was badly hurt in the battle…" Her voice cracked and she stumbled over her words.

Ralyn put a comforting hand on her shoulder. "Was it bad?"

Tears interfered with her ability to stay calm. "I thought he was dead. He was lying so still. His eyes were open, but they didn't see me…" She felt like collapsing as she buried her face in her hands. Part of the horror would never wear off. That image would remain in her heart and mind forever, whether or not he lived.

The moment had come. Ralyn plunged forward, fearing the worst. "And Evan?"

Katherine couldn't stop crying. How could she tell Ralyn? As horrible as Michael lying in a room somewhere in the castle, in pain and alone; it wasn't as bad as knowing there was no hope at all that she would see him alive again.

"Katherine? Tell me what happened to my husband." Ralyn's voice shook on the last word. She anticipated what her sister would say.

"He…Evan…I…" But she couldn't go on. Katherine felt her world was collapsing around her. Yes, the kingdom was saved. However, the person she loved most in the world was dying, and she had to tell her only living relative that her husband was…

"Dead?" Ralyn whispered.

A tearful nod from Katherine affirmed her greatest fears.

Ralyn stood still, unmoving for a moment. The tears started flowing down her cheeks little by little. "I told him it would happen. I warned him of the danger, but he said everything would be okay." A sniff. "He promised everything would be okay. He said God would take care of him! I was to meet him here today and he would come out of the gate to meet me…" Her hand reached toward the open gate. Her heart was breaking knowing that her husband would never walk out those doors. "He promised it would be okay."

Katherine's body racked with her sobbing. Even Ralyn's similar sorrow could not appease the pain in her heart. Michael was going to die. All their hopes and dreams and plans for the future would die with him.

She felt Ralyn's hand on her shoulder again. The baby started to cry. She could hear Ralyn trying to quiet the little one with soft sounds and whispers. "Shh, Helen. Mother's here. Shh. It will be alright."

It will be alright. The phrase echoed through her head and spat in her ears. *It will be alright? How can it be alright?* Her heart felt like it was breaking. The pain was too great.

Suddenly, real pain shot through her body. She screamed and bent over, clutching her stomach with both hands.

"Katherine! What's wrong? Katherine, answer me!"

She was too focused on breathing to answer. One breath in, one breath out. *Everything will be alright.* The echo seemed to laugh at her pain.

"Katherine!" Ralyn reached out and grabbed her wrist. "Katherine, answer me! What's wrong?"

A gasp accompanied her last conscious thought. "The baby…It's early."

Ralyn caught her sister with one hand as Helen screamed in her other arm. Katherine was breathing heavily and unconscious, passed out from the pain. Panic streaked through the young queen's body. She was about to lose her sister! She was going to die right here in her arms! Then she would be truly alone in the world. "God! Help her! Don't let her die!"

Suddenly, her brain understood Katherine's last muffled cry. "The baby! Katherine's baby?" Gently she put her hand on her sister's doubled up stomach. A soft kick met her hand halfway. "Katherine! Why didn't you tell me?"

Her next thought was that she not only had to keep Katherine alive, but this baby as well. "Someone help! Please help!"

KATHERINE'S KINGDOM: TO LOVE IN PEACE

The men were already ahead of her. They had heard Katherine's scream and sent someone to get Eli. When Ralyn finally put all the pieces together, he was running out of the gate. Adam and Edwin followed closely behind.

They gathered around Ralyn. Eli put his hand on Katherine's forehead. "She's burning up." A hand on her wrist. "Her pulse is racing." Before he could move another inch, Ralyn interrupted.

"It's the baby, Eli. She said it's early. How early is it?"

"I don't know. I only found out yesterday."

"Yesterday! How did you not know until yesterday?"

Eli shook his head. "She didn't tell anyone."

"Surely her husband…"

"Not even Michael knew. I think he suspected, but he never pushed it. I also suspected, but I didn't think she was this far along. She hid it well."

The unconscious Katherine felt the pain rocket through her body once again and moved, arched her back, and let out a cry.

Eli grabbed on of her arms. "We can't let her deliver this baby in a bloody battlefield! Adam help me!" The two men picked Katherine up and started to carry her to the castle. Edwin took the baby from Ralyn's arms and allowed her to run alongside Katherine's limp body, whispering comfort to her pain-filled heart and body.

How long had it been? This pain felt like it would never leave. Every so often she felt it get especially bad and somewhere in the blackness, she heard herself scream. Darkness enveloped her. "The baby?"

Ralyn's voice whispered to her. "It will be okay, Katherine. The baby's fine. You're fine. Eli and I are going to help you deliver this baby and it's going to be okay. Everything will be alright."

"Everything will be…alright." The darkness pulled her back again.

"Is she going to make it, Eli? Is she going to live?"

Eli was just as worried as Ralyn, but promised himself that he wouldn't let himself show it. "With God's help. With God's help, she will live."

The two watched and waited anxiously. Katherine remained unconscious.

Darkness was shifting. It felt as though a veil was being pulled from her eyes. Gradually, she could see the bedroom around her. The windows were open and the sun was shining brightly. Katherine turned her head to view the rest of her surroundings. To her right, Ralyn sat upright in a wooden chair. She was sleeping with her head leaned to one side.

"Ralyn?" Her voice sounded thin and wavering.

Her sister stirred and slowly half opened her eyes. When she saw that Katherine was awake, she fully awakened. "Katherine! I was so worried you would never wake up! You were so exhausted."

Katherine smiled. "The baby? Is the baby alright?"

Before Ralyn could answer, the door swung open with a slight creak. Eli came in just then, carrying a baby in his arms. Katherine let out a little squeak of joy and reached out her arms to hold the little one. With a smile that covered his whole face, Eli handed her the tiny bundle and whispered, "It's a girl."

Katherine looked down at the baby in her arms. Her tiny hands reached out to grab her mother's fingers. She was sleeping peacefully, with a half smile across her face. She had brown hair like her father.

"Does Michael know?"

Eli and Ralyn looked at one another before he slowly answered. "Michael has not regained consciousness."

Katherine clutched the baby closer to her chest. "Is he going to make it?"

"I don't know."

Silence. "May I see him?"

Ralyn started to protest. "You're not well enough to move yet, Katherine. Michael wouldn't want you to risk your health. Please rest at least another day."

KATHERINE'S KINGDOM: TO LOVE IN PEACE

"Michael may not have another day."

Eli thought for a few moments before answering. "You may see him, but not for very long. Take the little one with you. She will remind you to keep hopeful."

Before he could say another word, Katherine was out of bed. She handed the baby to Ralyn while she dressed and was soon out the door.

The room was dark. The windows were closed and the heavy winter curtains covered them. The bed was only big enough for one man. Eli had tried to find the most out of the way guest room for Michael. He didn't want prying eyes constantly harassing and prolonging the healing process. It was a good room for prayer. The darkness was so heavy that the baby started to sniffle and cry.

"You can feel it too, little one?" Katherine softly hummed until she went back to sleep. The presence of death was very near.

Michael looked so pale as he lay on the bed. His chest hardly moved as he breathed. His eyes fluttered under the lids. "Are you having nightmares, Michael?"

Of course, there was no response. She put her hand on his still cold one. "I know you can't hear me, but I just want you to know that I love you." She sniffed. "I'm sorry I didn't tell you sooner. I mean, I know you know that I love you, but…" Her voice trailed off as she lost the words to say. She rocked the baby in her arms for a few moments. Every motion reminded her of Michael. He should be here with her, holding his little girl and cooing to her. Telling her everything would be alright. Promising the world would look a little brighter tomorrow.

"I wish you could see her. She looks just like you. She's got your eyes and your unceasing smile. Do you know what I named her, Michael?" A pause. She watched his unresponsive face. "I named her Sophia." A sniff. "It means peace. That's what you wanted for her. To live in peace in Adven. To grow up not having to be afraid. I hope all that happens. I just hope you'll be there to see it."

Katherine paused her little speech. She looked around the room, trying to hold back the tears. She could feel little Sophia starting to tense up. The overwhelming heaviness in the room was almost too much for her to bear.

"It's so dark in here, Michael. I wish I could open the window." She thought for a moment. "Why can't I open the window?" With that thought uppermost in her mind, she flung back the curtains and opened the window. A slight breeze filled the room and the sunlight danced on the furniture, Sophia's sleeping face, and Michael's still form. The tenseness in the room instantly lifted. Darkness retreated to the corners and she felt hope stir in her heart again. "It's amazing what a little light can do!"

Sophia yawned and opened her eyes. She was such a calm baby. Her bright brown eyes squinted in the light; and she rubbed her tiny fists in them. Katherine smiled. "You really do bring hope to a person, don't you? You make me want to live forever, Sophia." She kissed the tiny forehead.

Michael still hadn't moved, except for the small rising and falling of his chest as he breathed. Katherine moved to the chair beside the bed. Eli must have been sitting there watching his patient, hoping he'd awaken. Now it was her turn for a little while.

"I don't know why God allowed this to happen. A few months ago I saw my father, dead on a battlefield. A few days ago, I saw my brother-in-law die the same way. I don't want to watch you die, Michael." She took a breath and with their daughter in one arm, placed her free hand on the bedside. "But I will. I promised to love you, and I won't ever break that promise. Love as strong as death. I never thought the death part would come so soon." The tears were coming again. It was so easy to cry these days! "But I won't give up. God gave me peace for the battle yesterday. I pray He'll give me peace for what lies ahead. And, I promise, I'll keep going. No matter what happens to you. I'll love you forever, Michael; but I'll love Sophia and rule Adven just the same. I may not understand why God does what He does, but I'll trust Him." She patted Michael's hand and stood to her feet. She gathered Sophia in her arms and pulled her close. Before she left, Katherine turned back to look at her husband. He was lying so still. His face was as white as a sheet. Nothing but his chest moved, up and down, up and down.

"Good-bye, Michael. 'Place me as a seal over your heart, like a seal on your arm; for love is as strong as death, its jealousy unyielding as the grave. It burns like blazing fire, like a mighty flame.' I'll love you forever, I promise."

The door was almost closed. Her tears were starting to fall down her cheeks. Sophia was beginning to fuss. Everything was falling apart. But then, that strange peace. She'd felt it right before the battle. She felt it every time God spoke directly to her. Everything was going to be okay. Somehow, everything was going to be okay.

"Katherine?"

It was in her head. It had to be. That couldn't be…

"Michael?"

She flung the door open and heard it crack against the wall. On the bed lay Michael, pale as ever. But something had changed. His hand was lifted off the bed ever so slightly. He was reaching for her.

"Michael!" Katherine rushed to the bedside and grabbed his hand. There was hardly a response to her touch, but she could feel warmth where before it was cold and lifeless. Sophia started to cry, clearly dissatisfied with the sudden change in movement and emotion.

His eyes fluttered open. "Is that her?"

Startled, Katherine looked oddly at her husband. "How did you know?"

A smile filled his face. "I've known for awhile. You're my wife. Don't you think I ought to know?"

"But, I didn't tell you! I was worried what you would think."

"I've felt her kicking during the night for some time now. I figured you were waiting for a good time to tell me."

Katherine blushed. "I was. But, then you started talking about having a family after the war. I knew that it was coming sooner than you hoped; and I just didn't know what to do."

Another smile. Michael opened his eyes and squeezed her hand. "All is forgiven. Let me see her."

She drew closer and held the still squirming bundle so he could see. "Her name is Sophia."

Michael smiled at the little girl in his wife's arms. She was getting ready for another cry and wrinkled her nose at her father. Her tiny fists swung around until they found a home halfway in their owner's mouth. Sophia sucked hard on her hand and settled back to sleep.

"She's beautiful."

Drawing back Katherine looked down and replied, "She looks just like you." A smile. "It's so good to have you back." Quickly, she planted a kiss on Michael's forehead and headed out the door. "I'd best go tell Eli the good news."

Chapter Twenty-Two

"Let me see her."

Katherine handed the fast growing Sophia to Michael's open arms. "It's hard to believe she's already a month old."

He flashed a smile before turning his attention to the little girl. "It's hard to believe we've managed to live in peace for a month after two years of nothing but war."

The couple was walking in the garden. The sun was shining and the grass was growing. Little flower buds were starting to open and present their beautiful colors to the world. Bluebirds and cardinals flew from tree to tree, collecting straw and twigs for their nests. Bright orange and yellow butterflies fluttered from flower to flower, drinking in the sweet nectar hidden within the colorful petals.

"How is Ralyn? I haven't seen much of her."

Katherine sighed. "She's grieving. Spends a lot of time with Helen."

"Is she avoiding me?" Michael's face was etched with concern.

"In some ways no." A shrug. "In other ways yes. You look just like Evan. Everything you do reminds her of him. Just being here in Adven reminds her of him, but going back to Suffrom would be too much for her." She stopped walking and touched Michael's shoulder. "I've been meaning to ask if she could stay here. It's going to be too hard trying to run Suffrom, raise Helen, and grieve all at the same time. I think Ralyn wants to forfeit her claim to Evan's throne."

"She shouldn't do that! Keep the title so that Helen has something to look forward to, other than living on the charity of her aunt and uncle. I can run both Suffrom and Adven. It's what would happen either way."

A smile. "Ralyn might be willing to compromise with that."

Sophia interrupted with a little cry followed by a yawn and a stretch. Her fist found it's way to her mouth and settled. Sleep was soon to follow. Her parents laughed.

"It's amazing how quickly she falls asleep," Michael said as he passed her back to her mother.

"I wonder who she gets that from," Katherine said as she wrapped the blanket tighter around the sleeping baby.

A splash from the fountain and water down the back of her dress met the remark. Michael stood looking mischievous as he dried his hand on his pants. Shocked, Katherine rushed to the fountain and splashed Michael, careful not to get Sophia wet. He wiped the water from his face and splashed her again. This time the water spilled onto a surprised Sophia, who cried in protest. Katherine retreated from the scene of the crime with a glare over her shoulder. Trying to look as innocent as possible, Michael caught up with her as they turned the corner and passed out of sight of Adam and Edwin, who'd been watching from behind a hedge. They laughed until they cried and walked in the opposite direction.

"Are Your Majesties sufficiently dried off?" Adam teased as he entered the dining hall. The couple was enjoying the last little bit of lunch as the servants washed dishes and scrubbed floors. Even chores felt fun when there was no threat of disaster waiting at the door.

"Adam! You were spying on us!" Katherine smiled as Michael choked. She laughed as her husband tried to compose himself instead of bursting into laughter. "Is that the example you have set for our counselors?"

"Laughing in the worst situation? Of course! What better trait could I teach him?"

A lone pea went flying at Michael, who ducked just in time. "Are you sure we're parents? I feel like I should be yelling at myself to stop playing with my food."

Adam laughed. "I believe you have a little while before Sophia is old enough to avoid her vegetables. Where is the little one?"

"With Ralyn and Edwin. Edwin is watching Sophia and keeping Ralyn company while she watches Helen."

"You left Edwin in charge of your heir?" Adam's smile betrayed him. He wasn't really surprised. Edwin had taken a shine to the tiny princess the moment he'd met her. The girl cooed and ceased to cry in his presence. There couldn't be a more perfect relief for Katherine and Michael. Every spare moment he got; he was spending watching Sophia. He'd make a perfect guardian if she ever felt the need to travel.

"You know very well that Edwin is perfectly capable of taking care of Sophia. Probably more qualified than Katherine or I."

"Speak for yourself, Michael!" The pea flew back at her. She laughed and picked up both plates. "I'd better get these to the kitchen before we start a full scale war."

"We've had enough of that," Adam added before he sat down at the table with Michael. Katherine drifted out of the room towards the kitchen. The king sat watching her until she was completely out of sight.

"Do you ever regret it?"

"Regret what?" Michael turned his attention to Adam's question.

"Marrying her. You could have stayed completely out of the war. Stayed healthy and uninjured. Been ruler of your own people. Never had to watch your brother die. Was it worth it?"

Without a second thought he replied, "Absolutely! There's no guarantee the war wouldn't have found us. We could have been easily overthrown if that madman had ever decided he wanted to destroy us. As for being ruler, I still am! But now, God has blessed me by providing me the opportunity to rule both Adven and Suffrom, neither of which would I have ruled had I stayed home." A pause. "Technically, I didn't watch Evan die, but I feel as if I did. Evan was my only brother, my big brother. He took care of me, watched me grow up, and was more of a father than my own father sometimes. It pains me to watch Ralyn mourn everyday. I pray that God will give her peace. He has already blessed me with an abundance of it."

"Of what?"

"Peace. Peace to know that no matter what happens everything will be okay. Peace to trust that God is in control. Peace to know that He will take care of my family, my country, and myself. It's that peace that overwhelmed Katherine when everything looked bleak. At the point when the world was crashing down on her, she put all her faith in God, giving up even her love for me. I love her so much."

Adam smiled and waited for Michael to continue.

"I guess that's what I would miss most. If I had stayed, I wouldn't have met Katherine. I wouldn't have married her. We wouldn't have a beautiful little girl. Ah, Sophia. She's the light of my life! What a miracle being a parent is! God is so gracious to allow us that experience. Just as He has adopted us into His family and become our Father; He allows us to experience the joy and sorrow of fatherhood."

Katherine came back in right at this moment and overheard the last phrase.

"Speaking of the joy of fatherhood, perhaps you'd like to rescue Edwin from Sophia? She's tired and doesn't want to sleep. Edwin and Ralyn have tried everything. Even Helen is becoming upset by her fussing."

Michael flashed a smile at Adam. "It would be my pleasure."

He grabbed Katherine and pulled her out the door, putting his arm around her waist and kissing her cheek as he did so. Adam shook his head. He smiled after the happy couple. "It was obviously worth it."

"Ralyn?"

The Queen was standing solemnly on the balcony of the guest room. She rocked the sleeping Helen in her arms and stared into the distance. Startled by the intrusion of her thoughts, she turned around. A slim smile spread across her face.

"Katherine. Did you and Michael finally get Sophia to sleep?"

"It took both of us. That little girl was determined that sleep would not win!" Katherine laughed and put her arm around Ralyn's shoulders. "And Helen?"

"Calm again. She doesn't like to be woken up." The smile faded. "She's like her father in that respect. He always waited until the last minute to get out of bed." Ralyn's eyes misted over as they looked out towards the horizon. "I'm going to miss him."

Katherine didn't know what to say. She almost understood, but Michael had lived against all odds! What kind of comfort was that to her sister, whose husband had died fighting in a war that wasn't even his own?

"I'm sorry, Ralyn. Is there anything I can do?"

"No. I don't suppose so." A sigh.

"You know we're willing to help in any way we can, right?"

"I know." Ralyn pulled away from her sister. Katherine frowned at her sister's back. She wasn't making this easy.

"Ralyn," she started. "Michael and I have been meaning to ask you what your plans are."

"I don't have any." Her voice sounded so empty, devoid of hope. "I suppose I should go back to Suffrom." She shook her head. "It will be very lonely without Evan."

Katherine moved closer to the grieving widow. "I know. That's why I asked Michael if you could stay here with us. Helen and Sophia could grow up together. You and I would be together. It would be like when we grew up."

"No, things will never be like when we grew up. Mother and Father are gone. We are both mothers. I've lost a husband." Her voice shook as she continued, "Things will never be the same."

"I know it won't be exactly the same. Things are different now." Katherine moved beside her sister. "Look! Everywhere you look there are people that have never heard the truth about God. A few years ago, they would never have had the opportunity." Joy filled her voice and she spoke faster and faster. "Now, they have a King and Queen that love God. We get to tell the whole kingdom! Someday Adven will be just like Suffrom, a place that serves the one true God."

Ralyn chanced a smile. "I look forward to that day, Katherine. You and Michael have a bright future ahead of you." She looked down at the sleeping baby in her arms. "I wish I could say the same for my little girl. If I stay here I will have to abdicate the throne. Michael will rule and I will be nothing but a widow in my sister's castle."

"No! You can remain the Queen! Michael will help you of course, he can travel much faster and more easily than you; but that way Helen will remain a princess and next in line for the throne. There can be a bright future for the both of you."

"I suppose." She stared with empty eyes across the vast landscape.

Katherine leaned close to her and whispered. "Don't give up hope. Trust God. Even when we don't understand what He's doing, we can trust Him. He knows what's best for both you and Helen. Everything will be okay."

"I hope so, Katherine. I hope so."

The sun slowly set. The days were grower longer and longer as spring rose to the height of its glory. Red, orange, and yellow rays of sunlight danced on the outside of the castle walls and the floor of the royal couple's bedroom. Katherine sat in the chair with Sophia in her lap, cooing softly. Michael stood looking out the window, watching the waning activity in the courtyard as the castle prepared for sleep.

Sophia yawned and stretched her tiny arms. The sound caused Michael to turn around and smile. "She is beautiful, isn't she?" He leaned down and kissed her on the forehead, then kissed his wife on the cheek. "Just like her mother."

"I spoke with Ralyn today."

"So that is why you've been so thoughtful tonight. You hardly spoke during dinner. Weren't Adam and Edwin's distractions enough to make you laugh?"

Laughter rang and tears ran down Katherine's face as she recalled the antics of the two men. "They certainly are something else. Where would we be without them?"

Michael's smile faded as he remembered the dark days of captivity. Even Katherine didn't know everything that had gone on during their forced separation. "Lost and alone." He shook the memory aside and the smile returned. "But God is good."

"Yes He is. I only hope that Ralyn remembers that."

"Is she considering denying her faith?" His arm rested on Katherine's shoulder and his face was etched with concern. "I thought that it was her greatest help when your mother died."

"It was for both of us. But this has been too much for Ralyn to bear. Just when life was going well for her, with a family to take care of and a kingdom to rule, everything changed. Evan's dead. She feels like God has betrayed her."

Michael squeezed her shoulder. "It sounds like you speak from experience."

She nodded and shivered a little, pulling Sophia closer to her. "I don't ever want to feel that way again. That's why I'm so worried about her."

"Everything will be okay. God is in control, even when we don't understand Him."

"I know." She handed Sophia to Michael and watched him as he carefully finished rocking her to sleep. "But I'm glad He gave me someone to remind every once and awhile." She kissed him and they stood together, husband and wife, enjoying the moment as a family.

Chapter Twenty-Three

It was another feast day, a celebration of peace. The dining hall was decorated with bright colors and fragrant flowers. The knights danced with their ladies and children ran in between their parents' legs. King Michael and Queen Katherine sat in their thrones on the raised dais. They watched the joy and laughter on their people's faces, enjoying every moment.

Adam and Edwin were goofing off together as usual. They laughed and talked with anyone who would listen to them. Their stories grew crazier and the songs louder, but today was a day for such things. The threat of war was past. Peace was reigning in the hearts and minds of the people. Fear was cast far away in places unheard of.

Little Lily was peering into the cradle where Princess Sophia lay. Her big brown eyes took in every new sight and sound while her fingers reached for a lock of Lily's hair.

"She's very pretty, Your Majesties."

Katherine smiled at her attempt to be polite. "Thank you, Lily. Would you like to hold her?"

The girl's eyes grew as big as the sun and sparkled like stars. "Can I? I won't drop her. I promise!"

Carefully, Katherine picked the child up and handed her to Lily. If it was possible, both Lily and Sophia's smiles grew. "I think she likes me!"

Michael bent down to put his arm around both Sophia and Lily. "I think you're right. Maybe you will get to help us take care of her. What do you think?"

Lily was speechless. After the shock passed, she said, "Could I really? I'll teach her how to cook and sew and read and climb trees and play…"

He interrupted the excited flow of talking. "Of course. And could you teach her one really important thing for me?"

The little girl nodded furiously.

"Teach her to love life as much as you do."

A tear slipped down Katherine's face. All of her fears seemed to not matter. Sophia had been born, a beautiful princess. The kingdom was free. Michael loved her more than ever. God really did have everything in control!

Lily smiled and held the little princess. "I can do that, Your Highness. Can I go tell my mom?"

"Of course." He took Sophia back and Lilly ran off through the crowd to tell her mother of her special mission for the king. Michael turned to see the solitary tear running down Katherine's cheek. He didn't say anything. He didn't have to. He saw the joy on her face and the peace in her heart. "Everything is okay." He brought Sophia to her mother and passed her to her open arms. "I love you."

"I love you too."

He leaned forward and whispered in her ear. "You are a seal over my heart."

She whispered back. "And I'll love you forever."

The two smiled and Sophia let out a loud squawk. Michael laughed and said, "We'd better start the ceremony. The princess is impatient."

He raised his hand for quiet. The laughter stopped and the talking subsided to a quiet hum. Adam and Edwin even stopped their foolishness and paid attention. The children were caught by their parents and made to stand still.

Michael smiled at the antics of the people before him. "It is great to stand here as your king, but also as your friend. It warms my heart to see your smiles and hear your laughter." A few giggles from the children. "We have made it!" Cheers erupted and he had to wait a few moments before he could continue. "God is good!" Even louder cheers echoed through the big hall. He raised his hands and let the smile on his face grow. Even Katherine was laughing.

"He deserves your praise, but I will never finish in time for the feast if I am unable to continue!" Silence immediately swept through the room. No one wanted to miss the feast that had been prepared in anticipation of this very day. "Today you are free, not only from your enemies; but you are also free from yourselves. I look at you and see just how many of you have put your trust in God. He has gained much from our trials, as have we. Where would we be without the lessons we have learned from these hard times?" A murmur of agreement.

"Today is a day of rejoicing and giving glory to God for what He has done." Cheers. "But," he paused, "there are others that we have to reward." Katherine stepped forward to stand beside her husband. Sophia squirmed in her arms.

"Adam."

The crowd made space in front of the raised dais for him to come forward. Adam walked to where he stood immediately before Michael. He drew his sword and laid it at his king's feet, then knelt.

Michael stepped forward again. "Rise." He rose. "You have been a good servant of your king. There is no reward that I could give to repay you for all you have done. You followed me from your home, in search of a new kingdom. You have given me good advice. You have helped to train those valiant knights who fought outside these very gates." Here he was interrupted by a cheer from the valiant knights. Adam smiled. "You have been one of my dearest friends." A pause.

"Therefore, I place you in charge of training all future knights of this realm. I personally charge you to train both Princess Sophia and Princess Helen in swordsmanship and warfare. Prepare them for their future roles as rulers of Adven and Suffrom. Also, you are to be one of my chief advisors in all matters." He leaned forward and whispered. "God bless you, my friend."

The people clapped their hands and cheered as Adam walked back to his place beside Edwin. The knights were the loudest, excited that their teacher would remain their teacher. Michael raised his hands for silence. "Edwin," he said when the crowd had quieted.

Nervously, the young man walked to the space in front of Michael. He also drew his sword and laid it at the king's feet. He knelt, but ran a nervous hand through his wild red hair as he did so.

Michael smiled. "Rise. You have nothing to fear." The crowd laughed and Edwin jumped to his feet. "You also have given much in the service of Adven. Though you were engaged in the army of the enemy, you sought to help us escape at all costs. You have not allowed your youth to stop you. You fought valiantly in the battle and singlehandedly saved the Queen's life." Cheers. Katherine smiled and Sophia cooed.

"In return for your sacrifice you are to be put in charge of that which you love. All horses of Adven are to be trained by you. I also wish you to teach the Princesses how to ride and any others who may wish to learn." Lily's happy squeak could be heard and little bits of laughter were heard all around the room. "You also are to be one of my chief advisors, a help in all circumstances."

Katherine stepped forward and bowed her head in a sign of respect. "Thank you, Edwin. You have saved me more than once, with no concern for yourself. You have indeed earned your reward. Thank you." She stepped back and Edwin blushed. He clumsily wandered back to his place. Adam clapped him on the back and the people clapped and cheered.

Michael stepped back and put his arm around Katherine's waist. She waited for the cheers to die down, then spoke up. "There is one more who deserves recognition." The people looked at each other and around the room. "Eli, will you come forward, please?"

The old man walked through the crowd with tears of pride welling up in his eyes. He knelt at the feet of the King and Queen. His bowed gray head almost seemed to shine in the shimmering sunlight. The room was absolutely silent, taking in the reverence of the moment.

Katherine stepped forward and handed the baby to Michael. He smiled and stepped back. Her eyes turned to look at the man who had been like a father to her all of her life. "Eli, please rise."

He stood.

Tears obstructed her voice as she continued to speak, "My dear, dear friend. You've been like a father to me. You've taught by example what it means to lead. You put up with all my childhood antics, forgiven all my mistakes, and tended to my wounded pride more often than not." Snickers from the crowd.

"But, do you know what you have done that meant more than anything else?"

"No. I do not, Your Majesty."

"You led the way for the people when I returned. It was you who first believed in God. Your example has opened the door for all the people you see before you." She swept her hand across the room. There were many tears and quiet nods of agreement everywhere she looked.

"I'm nothing but a foolish old man, Katherine."

She looked into his eyes with pure love in her voice. "A foolish old man who was willing to admit his foolishness and give it to God."

The crowd clapped and cheered. Joyful celebration filled the room. God was not someone who lived far away and only accepted their sacrifices to hear prayer. He was here, in the joy and happiness of this day and this moment. God was in this man who, by his own example, gave up what he knew to follow something different.

"I am honored by your words, Your Majesty."

Katherine drew her sword and held it in front of her. Hands on the hilt. Blade pointed toward the ground. It shone with God's presence as she held it. The light made her face shine like the sun. Her smile lit up the room and made the light grow. "You deserve great honor for what you have done. Eli, you are truly a hero of Adven."

With those words, she knelt on the ground. Every person in the room followed her example, even Michael with Sophia in his arms. Eli shook his shaggy head and raised Katherine to her feet.

"I am not worthy of such honor. Only God is."

Michael stepped forward. After Katherine sheathed her sword, he passed Sophia to her. Then he turned to Eli. "You have spoken wisely, my friend. Give honor to whom honor is due. We wish to give you the greatest honor we can." Katherine stepped forward again and placed Sophia in Eli's arms.

She said, "We wish to dedicate our daughter to God today. We wish that you would be her teacher in all of His ways. Train her in the knowledge of who He is and what He stands for. Lead her to know Him as we do. Will you do this for us?"

Eli stood silently sobbing for a moment, overwhelmed by the King and Queen's trust in Him. "I will," he said when he'd regained composure.

Michael nodded and then spoke. "We are grateful that you have accepted this charge. Know that we trust you implicitly. Your advice has helped us on many occasions. It is for this reason that I ask you to be my chief advisor. You, along with Adam and Edwin, will help Katherine and I in all of our decision making."

"I will do this also if that is what my king wishes."

Michael then turned to the people. "What you have seen this day has been a moment in the history of Adven. Know that we will never be the same! It is my wish to build a church where we may worship the One True God. As more of Adven comes to know God, we will build other churches. Let it be proclaimed that Adven will become a nation that follows God! That is the desire of both Queen Katherine and I. We pray that the kingdom has peace and prosperity for many years, so that we all may learn and grow together. Praise God for His goodness!"

The people cheered once more and celebrated even more than they had before. The children laughed and chased each other around the room, under tables and around chairs. People danced and sang, praising God with their voices. Many simply cried, completely overwhelmed. A new dawn had come for Adven and the darkness was being chased away even as Michael had spoke. Just like the love in Katherine's heart lit up her sword, the joy in the people of Adven lit up the room.

"And now," Katherine said with a laugh, "let the feast begin!"

The people flocked to the table and the cooks began to bring in all the food that had been prepared. Sophia had been placed in her cradle and slept soundly, worn out already from all the excitement of the day. Michael placed his arms around his wife's waist and pulled her close.

"Is it as you wanted? Adven will know God. The kingdom is at peace. Truly God is great."

"Yes. He is," Katherine said as she turned to kiss her husband.

The End

Would you like to see your manuscript become a book?

If you are interested in becoming a PublishAmerica author, please submit your manuscript for possible publication to us at:

acquisitions@publishamerica.com

You may also mail in your manuscript to:

**PublishAmerica
PO Box 151
Frederick, MD 21705**

www.publishamerica.com

PublishAmerica